When the Roxville Station cats had eaten and gone, Rachet stole to the feast—and found the cans empty. She pawed and nosed them and grew hungrier. As a crowd of people arrived to take the trains, she ran under the station platform and hid in a paper bag.

Just then a boy arrived. He loved cats but could not have one. No pets in his home!

He saw a yellow-and-orange cat disappear under the platform, as did the friendly man who took the 7:05 train every day.

"Mike," the man said when he saw Mike was watching the cat. "I guess we've got another cat to name. How about Tigre? She looked like a tiger."

"She looks more like a survivor to me," said Mike, glancing as she retreated under the platform. "Let's call her 'Rachet.'"

He got down on his knees and looked under the platform where Rachet had fled. She hissed in fear and warning, a double-meaning comment. Tucking her paws more tightly under her, she was ready to run. But she did not. She held her ground and growled at Mike instead. He laughed. Then she perked her ears up brightly. He got back to his feet.

"Sure wish I could have her," he said.

OTHER BOOKS BY
JEAN CRAIGHEAD GEORGE

My Side of the Mountain

On the Far Side of the Mountain

Frightful's Mountain

Dipper of Copper Creek

Charlie's Raven

The Wolves Are Back

Pocket Guide to the Outdoors

Jean Craighead George

The CATS
of Roxville Station

❖❖

ILLUSTRATED BY TOM POHRT

PUFFIN BOOKS
An Imprint of Penguin Group (USA) Inc.

PUFFIN BOOKS
Published by the Penguin Group
Penguin Young Readers Group, 345 Hudson Street, New York, New York 10014, U.S.A.
Penguin Group (Canada), 90 Eglinton Avenue East, Suite 700, Toronto, Ontario, Canada M4P 2Y3
(a division of Pearson Penguin Canada Inc.)
Penguin Books Ltd, 80 Strand, London WC2R 0RL, England
Penguin Ireland, 25 St Stephen's Green, Dublin 2, Ireland (a division of Penguin Books Ltd)
Penguin Group (Australia), 250 Camberwell Road, Camberwell, Victoria 3124, Australia
(a division of Pearson Australia Group Pty Ltd)
Penguin Books India Pvt Ltd, 11 Community Centre,
Panchsheel Park, New Delhi - 110 017, India
Penguin Group (NZ), 67 Apollo Drive, Rosedale, North Shore 0632, New Zealand
(a division of Pearson New Zealand Ltd.)
Penguin Books (South Africa) (Pty) Ltd, 24 Sturdee Avenue,
Rosebank, Johannesburg 2196, South Africa

Registered Offices: Penguin Books Ltd, 80 Strand, London WC2R 0RL, England

First published in the United States of America by Dutton Children's Books,
a division of Penguin Young Readers Group, 2009
Published by Puffin Books, a division of Penguin Young Readers Group, 2010

3 5 7 9 10 8 6 4 2

Text copyright © Jean Craighead George, 2009
Illustrations copyright © Tom Pohrt, 2009
All rights reserved

THE LIBRARY OF CONGRESS HAS CATALOGED THE DUTTON EDITION AS FOLLOWS:
George, Jean Craighead, date.
The cats of Roxville Station / Jean Craighead George; Illustrations by Tom Pohrt.—1st ed.
p.   cm.
Summary: Thrown into a river by a cruel human, a young tiger-striped cat fights to survive
amid feral cats and other creatures near Roxville train station, aided by Mike,
a fourteen-year-old foster boy who is not allowed to have a pet.
ISBN: 978-0-525-42140-5 (hc)
1. Feral cats—Juvenile fiction. [1. Feral cats—Fiction. 2. Cats—Fiction. 3. Animals—Fiction.
4. Human-animal communication—Fiction.]
I. Pohrt, Tom, ill. II. Title.
PZ10.3.G316Cat 2009
[Fic]—dc22   2008034217

Designed by Sara Reynolds

Puffin Books ISBN 978-0-14-241566-5

Printed in the United States of America

To Florence and Wendell
J.C.G.

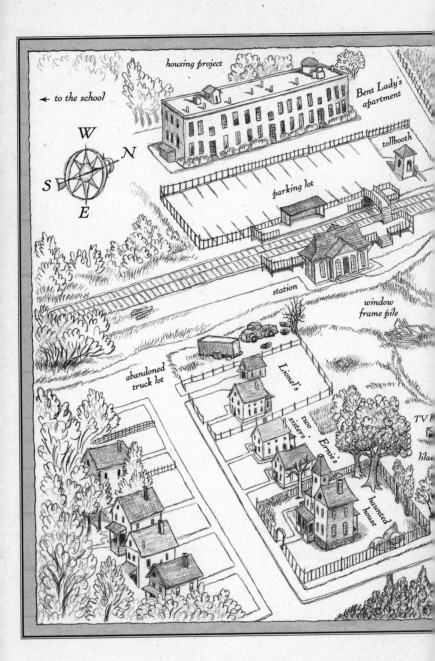

housing project

← to the school

Bent Lady's apartment

toolbooth

parking lot

station

window frame pile

abandoned truck lot

Lionel's

two sisters'

Ernie's

TV

lila

haunted house

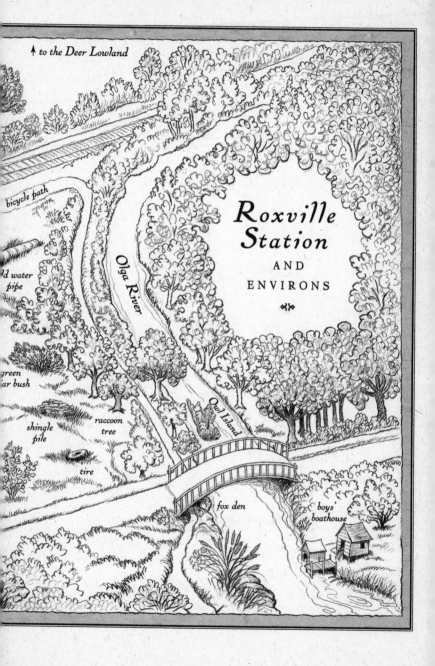

to the Deer Lowland

bicycle path

Old water pipe

green ar bush

shingle pile

raccoon tree

tire

Olga River

Roxville Station

AND ENVIRONS

Owl Island

fox den

boys' boathouse

The Cats of
Roxville Station

1

A lady in a fur coat threw a fighting, hissing cat off a bridge, got back into her car, and sped into the night.

Rachet the cat splashed into the river.

She felt the wetness, and hating it, reached out to claw this enemy. Her paw struck a stick, raked it for a better hold, and she was swimming.

An eddy caught her, swirled her shoreward until she felt stones under her feet and ran out of the water. Shaking her paws, she four-footed it into a woods that edged the river. When she was out of sight of the bridge she stopped, shook herself, and frantically licked the water off her sodden tiger-striped fur. With her forepaw she cleaned her ears of the river water, then her face and whiskers. The bruise on her ribs where the lady had kicked her yesterday had been soothed by the cold water and was no longer throbbing.

When she was almost dry, she crept deeper into the night woods. Rachet, like all cats, found her way in the dark with the rods in her eyes, which could take in the faintest of light, even starlight, and make the night into day. Smelling dryness, she hurried to the fallen leaves under an oak tree and frantically rolled in them. Then, shivering with loneliness and fright, she miaowed in her baby voice to bring her mother. There was no answer. Her world had changed.

With her whiskers feeling for obstacles and her nose smelling for living things, she cautiously walked down a well-trodden path. The path held the odor of the red fox, Shifty, but being young and inexperienced, Rachet did not know that red foxes hunted cats. So she followed his path to the edge of the woods.

There she stopped to look for and avoid people. The ones she knew kicked, picked her up by her orange-striped tail, or locked her in a closet without food or water when they went away for several days. She had been a plaything for children. Now, with summer over and the children back in school, the lady had dropped her in the river, hoping she would drown.

But Rachet was a cat. She had survived the kicks and closets and would survive this. With her feet poised to run at the sight of a human, she studied the scenes presented to her. An overgrown field of grasses, goldenrod, milkweed, and ragweed covered the two acres of abandoned farmland that lay in front of her. It was scattered with papers and discarded junk. The field ended at the Roxville railroad station, now under a rising moon. A few people were waiting on a platform for the puffing, whistling diesel trains to take them to the city. The people smelled acrid.

Just across the tracks from the station was a parking lot and beyond that, a housing project and a few businesses. A road and a sidewalk lay to her left.

Opposite her, several oily-smelling trucks were parked in an abandoned lot. Across the field next to the trucks were the backs of modest homes. On the corner stood a large Victorian house that was neglected and run-down. Behind her flowed the Olga River, out of which she had just swum.

Rachet sat still to orient herself, using her extraordinary cat sonar. Nearby were chipmunks, a raccoon in a tree, and farther away, some people walking on the sidewalk.

Suddenly she sensed two female cats hunting in the field and a tomcat, Volton, under the Olga River Bridge downstream of her. She would avoid them—especially those two female cats. Cats were to be kept at a respectable distance according to the ancient laws of the solitary domestic cat.

Holding her body low to the ground, her starchy

white whiskers out, she slinked away from the female cats, slowly at first, so as not to attract their attention, then faster and faster.

One of them saw her—Queenella, so named by the people waiting for trains at the station because she walked with her head and tail up and seemed to reign over the other cats.

Queenella came toward Rachet, striding elegantly down her Queenella trail, her very own highway in the grasses. Rachet arched her back. Her tiger fur rose to make her look bigger and therefore more threatening than she was.

Queenella surveyed the small puffed tiger cat, first with that one eye in a black patch of fur and then with the other in a patch of white. Holes in her ears marked fights with vicious rats, and a scar across her nose told of a past encounter with Windy, the barn owl. She could see that the stranger cat was marked with stripes. Cats see no color, just shades of gray, but the grays are colorful to them.

Queenella's black pupils nearly filled her green irises, expressing anger. She crouched and looked away, tilting her head slightly. That head movement warned Rachet that she was on Queenella's property and that she, Queenella, would fight for it. Through her whiskers and nose, ears, and eyes, Rachet learned that the big black-and-white cat, Queenella, was the high-ranking one—the boss cat.

Rachet backed up. Queenella came on, tail twitching, head tilted, watching her. Rachet knew cat "war" talk, though she had never seen it before in her six months of life. It was born in her.

Frightened, she leaped off the fox's trail into the rag-weed, dashed behind a yellowing goldenrod, and stared at Queenella, who calmly turned and walked away. The battle was over. Queenella had won. Rachet, the intruder, was off her territory.

Frightened, Rachet wedged into an abandoned automobile tire and, her heart racing, sat still until her fear odor vanished. The fear odor was strong and carried on the wind to Queenella, who hissed pleasurably. She had thrown respect into this youngster who was trying to join the proud group of independent, feral cats of Roxville Station. Queenella trotted off to the neglected Victorian house, known as the "haunted house" to the people on the block, dropped into a window well, and entered the basement through a broken pane.

Rachet catnapped to regain her nerve. Her new surroundings were not as threatening as another cat—not even the noisy cars and the people.

When at last she opened her large green eyes she saw that the tire was torn in places and that grass had grown through the holes. That was good. She scratched some of the dead grass into a pile, shaped it round and nest-like with her body, and curled up. Now, warm and well hidden inside the tire, she slept again, this time deeply.

When she awoke the sun was dawning through gray clouds. She licked herself again to get rid of the last faint odor of the lady in the fur coat and thought about food.

A blade of grass twitched just outside the tire. Rachet instinctively drew her feet under her and studied the grass through the tear in the tire. It quivered—something alive. Her hunger told her—mouse. Her tail twitched, her rear end went up, her chest lowered, and she pounced, swinging an open-clawed paw—and missed.

The mouse ran. It scurried down its trail and dove under a soda can. Rachet ran after it but only so far. Sitting down behind a clump of grass, she waited, motionless, for the mouse to come out and go home.

The ground shook, and a train roared into the station. She remained still and listened. Moments later a man's voice shouted "All aboard!" The mouse took advantage of the sound and scurried into its nest in the ground.

With its disappearance Rachet felt really hungry. She sniffed. But she didn't smell mouse. She smelled more cats crossing the vacant lot.

Queenella was first. Well behind her, running short distances, then stopping, came Ice Bucket, a white

but dirty cat. Next came Flea Market. Her brown fur
was matted from biting fleas. A small calico, Elizabeth, came slinking low from the vacant lot. She crept
daintily and shyly. Then came Tatters and Tachometer,
sisters. They dashed out from under the old tollbooth
at the entrance to the station parking lot, where they
had made their First Home after the parking meters
had been installed and the booth abandoned. All cats
seek a First Home, the place to which they return again
and again, be it a pillow by a fire, a corner of a couch,
or a sheltered spot in the wilds. It is not necessarily a
permanent place, for a cat will shift homes according
to food supply, mood, and events. Sometimes one will
change First Homes just for a cat whim.

All the cats were walking to the railroad station. Their
inner alarm clocks told them it was 6:45 A.M.—the time
the Bent Lady put out cans of cat food by the station
platform. She came there every day to feed the cats of
Roxville Station. She liked them better than the people
in the housing project, who rarely spoke to her. The cats
liked her, too. They meowed and said hello by bumping
their foreheads against her trousers.

Rachet smelled the food—the kind of food from a

can she had sometimes been fed. Its aroma piqued her hunger, and the hunger drove her forward. Boldly she joined the cats on their trek to the Bent Lady's hand-out—stopping and starting to keep out of their sight. Near the station platform she sat down and watched Ice Bucket and Flea Market approach the food. Their tails were up, not quite as high and straight as Queenella's, and they swished them to express their wariness of the queen.

In front of Rachet behind a pile of old window frames Elizabeth, the calico, crouched. Hidden, she was waiting for her chance to eat. Shy and low in rank, she watched.

Tatters and Tachometer ran confidently across the tracks and, tails up but bent at the tip to show defer-ence to Queenella, grabbed a bite and ran a distance away to eat. When they had enough they took their trail back to their shared First Home.

Finally Elizabeth nervously ran to the cans with her belly close to the ground, her tail almost dragging. She ate the leftovers and sped back to her First Home in the abandoned truck on the vacant lot.

The tomcat Volton, whose scent had been at the bridge, did not appear. He was headed for another group of feral cats out on a farm. Volton, like all male feral cats, wandered from cat city to cat city, visiting the females and fighting with other tomcats. Rachet accepted him as part of this new life.

When the Roxville Station cats had eaten and gone, Rachet stole to the feast—and found the cans empty. She pawed and nosed them and grew hungrier. As a crowd of people arrived to take the trains, she ran under the station platform and hid in a paper bag.

Just then a boy arrived. He was on his way to school

via the stairs over the tracks and through the parking lot and housing project. He went this long way to watch the cats that the woman known only as the Bent Lady fed. He loved cats but could not have one. No pets in his home!

He saw a yellow-and-orange cat disappear under the platform, as did the friendly man who took the 7:05 train every day.

"Mike," the man said when he saw Mike was watching the cat. "I guess we've got another cat to name. How about Tigre? She looked like a tiger."

"She looks more like a survivor to me," said Mike, glancing as she retreated under the platform. "Let's call her 'Rachet.'"

"Okay. She does look 'rachety,' whatever that is," he said.

"I sure wish I could have her. I love cats. They're so special."

"Offer her a can of cat food and you can," the man said. "No one owns her. She's a feral cat."

"My foster mother won't let me have a cat. She hates them," Mike said.

He got down on his knees and looked under the platform where Rachet had fled. Her eyes shone like green gems from inside the bag. She hissed in fear and warning, a double-meaning comment. Tucking her paws more tightly under her, she was ready to run. But she did not. She held her ground and growled at Mike instead. He laughed. Then she perked her ears up brightly. He got back to his feet.

"She's a scrappy one," he said to the Bent Lady and the man, his face lighting up.

He dusted off his baggy pants.

"Sure wish I could have her," he said again.

The train pulled into the station. The man climbed aboard, and the Bent Lady departed. When it pulled out Mike jumped off the platform, threw his backpack over his shoulder, and trotted off to school.

Rachet said something to me in cat talk, he mused, *and it wasn't "I'll fight if you pick me up." Her ears were perked pleasantly—those ears said something.*

Mike was pondering this as he entered his classroom and sat down at his desk. The other students chatted amiably with one another, but Mike didn't join them.

He had his elbows on his desk and his head resting in his hands—thinking. *I want Rachet. I like her. And I think she likes me.*

As he daydreamed, Rachet came out from under the platform and darted to the field on the other side of the tracks, tail straight out behind.

2

Still hungry, Rachet ran all the way to the tire and dove in.

She turned as smoothly as flowing water, lifted her head, and breathed in deeply. The Roxville Cats were each back in their First Homes. She could locate everyone but Elizabeth. Elizabeth was somewhere in that abandoned lot. But where? She sought her with her whiskers and nose and finally sensed her in the front seat of a junked truck.

When she had located everyone but Shifty, she went out to hunt anything that moved—bird, mouse, or frog. No sooner was she outside the tire than she sensed Shifty. The red fox was asleep near the mouth of his den under the bridge. Rachet was safe.

With her body in a crouch, her tail stretched out straight behind her, and her whiskers bowed forward to feel the vibrations of living things, she crept silently through the dying goldenrod.

Grasses moved. A mouse gleaning seeds took form as it ran. It was near the burrow of its den, and cat wisdom told Rachet to make herself invisible by sitting still.

The mouse finished the seeds and, still hungry, went down his grass highway, looking for more. A caterpillar diverted his attention, and Rachet tucked her hind legs under her, aimed her unsheathed forepaws, and pounced. She slammed down upon the mouse with deadly accuracy, felt it in her grip, but did not bite with her powerful jaws. Instead she lifted one paw out of curiosity—and it got away. She was racing after it when Shifty, out of his den now and right behind her, leaped on her yellow-and-orange tail. Screaming and hissing, she ran, dove in her tire, turned around, and spit. Shifty, she now understood, was more than a citizen of wild Roxville—he was an enemy. Her bleeding tail twitched in pain, and she licked it tenderly. Shifty did not come after her. He saw much easier prey in her wounded mouse and caught it in one graceful leap, his white tail tip held aloft. Shifty swallowed the mouse, then trotted off.

All day Rachet stayed in the tire. In the evening she came out, smelled Shifty nearby, and went back in. Somewhat later, when Shifty was down by the river, she stared out of her tire hole again, only to smell the red-headed boy, Mike, coming through the milkweeds toward her. He walked slowly, quietly, a flashlight in hand.

"Kitty, kitty," he called when he was almost upon the tire. She drew back farther but not so far that she couldn't see him.

"Here, kitty, kitty. Are you there?" He really wanted her. There was something magical about that cat.

Rachet, for her part, was strangely attracted to the boy and yet afraid of him. He was a human after all. She bowed her whiskers forward to sense him, could not, and curled up in the tire and slept.

Several days passed without food, and Rachet was

ravenous. She climbed out of the tire late in the afternoon and scanned the field. Something moved in a cluster of old milkweeds. A mouse? She stalked it. But it wasn't a mouse. It was a butterfly emerging from its chrysalis that was hanging from a dried leaf. Rachet watched it pull its six black legs out of the chitin box in which it had been changing from caterpillar to butterfly for the past two weeks. She gathered her feet under her for a pounce, but suddenly the tan creature shook its nubbin wings. They filled with fluid and expanded. The orange-and-black wings grew like a Japanese water flower. In moments Rachet was looking at a monarch butterfly. The cat in her wanted to play with this creature, but instead she purred. She purred only in the presence of a living creature, be it just a butterfly.

This pleasant purr filled the butterfly's world. It had no ears, but it felt the vibrations on its antenna and lifted its wings. The young butterfly hesitated, then took a bearing on the angle of the sun's rays and flew off. It was on a ruler-straight line for Mexico. As it went it would fly around buildings and tall obstacles and come back to that straight-line course until it finally arrived in the mountains of Mexico. Hanging from a pine needle, it would spend the winter with millions of other monarch butterflies that had migrated from North America, making the mountainside glow.

Watching it fly over the dried milkweed patch, Rachet was aware of a slight tremor in the grass nearby and pounced! She had a mouse.

This time holding it tightly in her teeth, she carried the mouse back to her tire and ate. It was delicious. She could hunt. She would live.

Rachet curled up tightly in the tire and closed her eyes. At dusk she went out prowling again.

She did not go very far before a storm blew in from the south, bringing rain. Cheeks, the chipmunk, stopped gathering acorns at the first drops and ran to his home in a stone pile by the bridge. He took a trail he had made through and around the rocks, went down a long tunnel in the earth below them, and stopped in his pantry. He stored his acorns, then scrambled down his runway for a visit to his tidy latrine. When the rain began to fall heavily he was in his bedroom/living room.

Mike, who headed home still looking for Rachet, climbed over his fence and ran up the back steps of the Victorian house where he lived. It was known as the "haunted house." An older woman, Mrs. Dibber, lived there. Before her husband had died of cancer two years ago, she had taken in Mike, who was then an eleven-year-old orphan. The state paid her for fostering him, and he did the chores.

Rachet did not sense him, for she was listening to a swish in the grass. The swish grew louder and closer. Fang, the snake, was pressing down hard on his belly scales as he slid under her tire. Inherited instinct warned her not to catch him, although he moved tantalizingly. Some programmed cat message said he was not poisonous but a common milk snake. Rachet nevertheless was cautious. He could bite. As she pulled away from him she saw the same butterfly hanging upside down and perfectly dry on the underside of a leaf. It had felt the low pressure of the storm and retreated under the foliage.

The rain pelted Roxville for hours. It deluged the abandoned field and woods and ran down the stem of the burr weed by Rachet's tire. The burr weed grew heavy, bent over, and poured water into the tire. A puddle formed there, growing bigger and bigger. Rachet pulled away from the hated wet. She must find a drier home.

She recalled what she knew of the north end of Roxville and, despite the odor of Shifty, sensed she must go under the bridge. It was dry and snakeless. She was about to dash for it when Fang slithered out from under the tire, also looking for higher ground. He flashed his tongue and tasted her chemicals on the air. The chemicals were a snake's word for *cat*.

He pinned her with his glassy stare.

The snake's eyes paralyzed her. Rachet could not

move. Fang, like all snakes, held prey motionless with
eyes that did not blink. Frogs and mice were unable
to run away, and Rachet, a cat, froze for an instant.
Because it was dark, she could look away and break the
hypnotic stare. Released, she ran for the bridge despite
the downpour. The snake slid back under the tire.

At the bridge Rachet smelled the strong and lemonish
odor of Shifty. He was at the entrance of his den above
Cheeks, the chipmunk's rock pile, watching the storm
in dry safety. Suddenly he picked up the buttery smell
of Rachet, ran out of his lair, and glided toward her.
Rachet felt him, left the dry protection of the bridge,
and ran to the old maple tree. Shifty followed, ignoring the rain. He was hungry. Frantically Rachet dug
her claws into the wet bark and climbed above Shifty,
then slipped and slid back down on the rain-slick bark.
Shifty's white teeth gleamed. Rachet dug her claws
deeper, climbed, discovered a hollow, and dove in.

Shifty saw that his prey was out of reach and ran
through the rain to his bridge den.

Rachet relaxed.

Then something moved in the hollow of the maple
tree.

3

It was Ringx, the raccoon. Not knowing if Ringx was an enemy like Shifty had turned out to be, Rachet climbed out of the deep hollow and onto a limb. Being a young cat, she knew how to climb up a tree but not how to get down. She stared at the ground below and miaowed the helpless kitten cry for mother, but in vain.

Ringx heard Rachet's cry and came from deep in the hollow to peer at the cat. Her beady eyes gleamed in a black furry mask, and her ears were laid back. Rachet took one look at the growling bandit face and leaped. She crashed through the tree limbs, grabbed one, couldn't hold on, and dropped twelve feet to the ground. Landing on all fours, she ran under the bridge and climbed up into the steel supports. On a high beam twenty feet up, she spit. With that adult cat comment, she discarded the kitten in her and grew up. No more miaows.

She was on her own amid people, storm, snake, fox, and raccoon. She stayed high on the bridge infrastructure until the rain let up. It was already very late at night when she stirred. She could hunt now. This is the time cats operate secretly and best—but so do Shifty and Ringx.

Below her two mice came out of the papers and junk. They searched the debris for tasty garbage the swollen Olga River had washed ashore from the parks and towns upriver. Rachet riveted her eyes on the mice. When they ran into a sodden paper bag, she jumped from arch to beam. They came out. She stopped. They disappeared. She ran. When she had worked her way down to the ground, she crept, body low, to a rock near them and sat still. By sitting stone-still and then running, she inched closer to the mice without their realizing she was there. Then suddenly with a flash of her paw she caught one. This time she did not lift it in curiosity but carried the food up to her spot on the steel beam and dined.

Another mouse took its place—then another. Rachet

had found a cat smorgasbord in the heart of fox and raccoon territory. She would need all her cat wits to mouse here with Shifty and Ringx around.

After she had eaten, she washed her mouth with her tongue, then her cheeks and the back of her neck with her paw. There she found a burr. Scratching it with her hind foot, she dislodged it. It fell into the water and floated with the current to a tidal cove.

A sparrow picked it up and flew landward. Suddenly chased by a hawk, the bird veered and dropped the burr. There it would lie all winter. When spring came it would send out roots and leaves and make more burrs to be dispersed by animals. Burrs were hitchhikers. Rachet had given it a ride from the field to the river to a bird, then from a flying bird to a new home. Rachet was unaware of her part in the burdock's scheme to spread burdocks. High on the scaffolding, she sat sphinxlike and catnapped.

Nights later, when a half-moon was riding like a ship through the clouds, Shifty left his den and wandered up the river shore, hunting. Rachet was awakened by his odor and sensed him until his smell disappeared.

Then she leaped down from the infrastructure and caught another mouse.

She ran toward the tire with it. All was well. Shifty was far upriver, Ringx had rambled to the Dumpsters in a nearby park, and Fang was frogging in the tall phragmites grass by the water. With that knowledge, Rachet was able to return to her tire with a mouse dangling victoriously between her front legs.

She stopped at the hole she had used to get into the tire. It was not only still puddled with water but also buzzing with mosquitoes. One female lit on the stagnant surface and deposited her eggs right under Rachet's nose. Other females whined around her face, looking for a furless spot to bite.

Rachet heard the insects, and repelled by the high pitch of the song, hopped to the top of the tire. Her green eyes scanned the field for a dry place to make her home and her ears shot up, listening for the emptiness of an isolated space. She saw and heard none, but she did hear other sounds—bats flying overhead and a nighthawk circling to find its direction before heading for a plateau in Argentina for the winter. Then a mosquito tried to alight on her nose and bite. The mosquito needed to take blood from a warm-bodied animal in order to form her eggs, and Rachet's naked nose was perfect.

Rachet batted at the mosquito while sensing where she could live in these suburbs. Foxes, deer, raccoons, skunks, turkeys, and birds lived here, so why couldn't she? They had homes among the wonderfully sloppy people who dumped food all around. These people were not hunters. A mother deer and her two fawns were proof of this. They walked casually through the moonlit woods on their way to eat the last hosta plants in the yards of the houses not far from the haunted house. Rachet could find a place here, too.

WHAM! The barn owl, Windy, her silent wings outspread, her feet low like a landing airplane's wheels, knocked Rachet off the tire and into the grass. Swooping up to the limb of a tree, the owl turned to strike again, but Rachet had dived inside the tire and was standing in the cold water. Windy did not wait for her to come out. She saw Rachet's mouse in the grass, winged down, and picked it up. Carrying it to a limb of the raccoon tree, she ate it in owl fashion—whole, and swallowed head first.

Here was another enemy, and this one was from the sky. Rachet stood in the cold water, now knowing that injury came from above as well as from land. She waited until Windy flew into the woods and the birdy smell of owl had disappeared. Then she stepped out of her tire, flipped the water off her paws, and crouched in the grass. It had been a long night.

At 6:45 A.M. her internal clock told her it was time
for the cat food and the trains. She got up, sensed Shifty
in his den, Ringx in her hollow tree, and Fang still in
the phragmites grass. Windy was in the shelter of the
cliffs along the Olga River. Rachet stepped forward.

She was not hungry but wanted to see the boy. She
did not know why. She was both afraid of and enthralled
by him. He was human, after all, and her experience
of humans had left her wary. But this boy seemed different.

The other cats knew it was feeding time, too. At that moment Queenella came out of the basement of the haunted house and took her highway to the train station.

Ice Bucket, an even dirtier white from mud and rain, awakened in a new First Home in an empty television box in the field. Cats love boxes and bags, and Ice Bucket had dived into this one upon seeing it. She *had* to. Now, feeling and listening, she stole out of the box and ran toward the cat food.

Flea Market emerged from a discarded piece of water pipe, her First Home, and Elizabeth came into the field from the abandoned truck lot. She hid from Queenella behind the stack of broken window frames and waited for her chance to eat.

The Bent Lady had already put out one can. Tatters and Tachometer left the tollbooth and ran silently to the station. They halted at the platform edge to judge the scene. Queenella was eating her can of cat food while watching the other cats. When she had her head in the can, Tatters ran up to the Bent Lady and rubbed her head against her leg to say hello. The Bent Lady as usual opened another can for the lower-ranking cats.

It was morning again at Roxville Station. People were waiting for the train.

"I wonder where the tiger cat is?" Mike asked the Bent Lady.

"Over there by those sodden newspapers," she said. "She's watching Queenella."

The Bent Lady had seen the new cat and opened a third can of food. She placed it in the grass at the far edge of the platform away from Queenella.

"Kitty, kitty," she called to Rachet.

Out of some species memory, that "kitty, kitty" song brought pleasure to Rachet. Enchanted, she dashed past Elizabeth hiding behind the window frames and stood before the cat food. Queenella snarled and tilted her head.

That tail swish and head tilt were "battle talk." Rachet did not run. Instead she fought back by thrashing her tail. Queenella saw Rachet's answer, growled again, and resumed eating. That growl had said to Rachet, "I'll let you stay, but I am queen." Rachet thrashed her tail again.

With that gesture she joined the Cats of Roxville Station as a ranking cat and could now eat. By standing up to Queenella, Rachet had moved herself up the cat social ladder. She now held a rank above Elizabeth of the abandoned truck lot. All the cats of Roxville Station knew this. They were working for the same rise in power. It organized them and made life easier, by preventing constant fights.

Ice Bucket walked over to Queenella's now deserted food can, and Elizabeth stole in beside her, ears down submissively. She sneaked food from Rachet's can while Rachet was chewing.

Tatters and Tachometer stole to the can where Ice Bucket was eating. They knew she tolerated them and would not fight. Cats respect one another but would rather not be good friends or too close.

Suddenly all the cats ran off and Rachet had the cans to herself—and then she knew why. Stalin, the hound from nearby, big, muscular, and poorly trained, was charging her, jaws open.

"Stop! Stalin, stop!" roared Mr. Vinski, Stalin's owner and Mike's neighbor. He was running after the dog, trying to grab his broken leash. They had been on their regular morning walk in the woods when Stalin

had lunged after a squirrel and broken away. The squirrel went up a tree, then the dog saw all the cats at the cat food and ran for them. They scattered—all but Rachet, who was ignorant of dogs.

Mr. Vinski, too preoccupied to hail Mike, caught up with Stalin. He clutched his collar and held on.

"Heel, heel!" he yelled. Stalin didn't heel; instead he pulled Mr. Vinski along as he ran for Rachet.

Spitting and hissing, she raised her fur until she was a spectacle of fury—a Halloween cat. Stalin lunged, but before his jaws could crunch her, Rachet, now a ball of frenzy, was clawing at him. She raked his nose. He howled and dove for her neck. Rachet jumped aside on all four feet and hissed.

Seeing that the fight was going to be unfair—little cat, big dog—Mike jumped off the station platform and threw his backpack between dog and cat. They stopped fighting. The people waiting for the train cheered the little cat.

Rachet was so stunned that she let Mike pick her up and carry her away from Stalin. Mr. Vinski was pulling firmly on Stalin's collar and dragging him back. Rachet looked up at Mike.

"Meow," she said.

For the first time she spoke cat language meant only for humans. It was not the "miaow" that a kitten emits to bring its mother, but "meow"—a straightforward statement and full of meaning. Cats hiss, spit, and growl to one another, but Rachet had spoken in an ancient language that cats have evolved to speak to humans. She did not reason why.

Mike looked down at her wide green eyes. They met his warm brown ones and he smiled. Rachet drew in her claws.

"Look," Mike said to the Bent Lady. "Rachet's eyes talk. When she was fighting Stalin, her pupils were huge. They were black and filled her irises. When I picked her up they grew narrow and she meowed."

"She trusts you," said the Bent Lady.

"Gee, I would like to have her," Mike said softly.

Rachet felt loving hands stroke her fur. For a moment she knew what it meant to be a house cat—a strange combination of usefulness and comfort that did not include ownership, for cats cannot be owned like dogs. Then she remembered that people kicked and people like this boy were rough. Tensing her muscles, she leaped out of Mike's arms, ran back under the platform and into a paper bag. Just then the train roared into the station, and the people on the platform boarded.

Peering out of the bag, she stared at the train wheels circling slowly, then fast and faster until the mammoth was gone. Then she saw Mike.

He was hanging over the platform, looking for her. He did not see her and stood up.

"That was some cat-and-dog fight," he said to the Bent Lady and picked up his backpack. They went to the bridge that crossed over the tracks, then off in separate directions, he to school, she to the housing project.

4

The loud train noise stopped Stalin from barking for an instant, and he watched it pull out. His diverted attention gave Mr. Vinski enough time to get control of him and snap on the leash. Stalin looked from the vanishing train to where the cat had disappeared and barked. Mr. Vinski pulled the dog toward the woods to resume their walk. The cats of Roxville Station watched.

Rachet stayed under the platform, safe from people and dogs, but still feeling Mike's fingers stroking her fur. She closed her eyes in pleasure. Something magical had happened.

Stalin and Mr. Vinski were on the bicycle path in the woods and all was quiet, so Rachet dashed over the tracks to the field. She slipped through the weeds without rustling them and took her own catwalk to the tire.

Rachet heard the crickets making cricket music as they rubbed their wings with their feet. Their songs were slow, which said it was forty-seven degrees Fahrenheit and that winter was coming—the slower their stridulations, or fiddling, the colder the weather. Above the cricket weather report Rachet heard cat paw beats. Volton was in town. He was following Elizabeth in courtship.

Rachet returned to her tire, only to find it still deep in rainwater. She must find a dry First Home, but right now she needed rest after the frightening morning. She smelled Fang sunning on the rocks near Cheeks the chipmunk's den and took his hiding place in the hollow under the tire.

At dusk she awoke, ready to go First Home hunting. She looked toward the abandoned lot where mice abounded. Elizabeth's First Home was there, and her Sunning Spot was on the nearby woodpile. Rachet wouldn't look there nor in the pile of brush in the field, Elizabeth's Hunting Lookout. She had sprayed it with her personal odor to tell other cats it was hers. Rachet respected this. The Sunning Spot and Hunting Lookout were stations in a cat's environment that it selected and regularly used.

Rachet inhaled deeply and smelled the two Roxville cat members at the faraway tollbooth in the station parking lot on the other side of the tracks. Tatters and Tachometer had left strong scents on it by rubbing their sides against the pilings as they exited and entered their home. The scents said, "This is Tatters and Tachometer's property." Rachet would stay away from their space also.

The woods were no good; they were claimed by Ringx. The raccoon lived in that large hole in the maple tree and protected it with ferocity. Lysol, the skunk, denned under a nearby slash pile. She did not want her First Home near him.

Rachet crawled out from under the tire and was stealing down her trail to check for a home near the houses when Shifty, the red fox, caught wind of her. Running low, then leaping high, he pounced with open jaws. Rachet sped through the withered thistle patch, Shifty at her heels. He was so close she heard his jaws slam closed. She leaped, aiming for a hole in

a mesh fence, went through it, and alit in the yard of
the big Victorian house where Queenella made her
home. Shifty was too wary to follow through the hole
and skidded to a halt. He sniffed the fence, then trotted away.

Old and run-down, the house had a large porch that
wrapped around two sides of it. The porch stopped at a
tower three stories high, then continued on the other
side. Stained glass glowed in the living room windows.
Elaborate leaves and flowers, moldy from neglect, were
carved above the windows and doors. Rachet looked
about the yard. In it were motorboats covered with
blue tarps; weeds grew between them. Slender volun-
tary saplings cropped up here and there at the fence.
Old sugar maple trees at the edge of the yard were rid-
dled with holes, showing where woodpeckers and flick-
ers had drilled. A sign in the yard read OCCUPIED, in
case someone thought the run-down house was empty
and decided to explore it.

Rachet took a deep sniff. The old house smelled of
people—and Queenella! Suddenly, Windy, the barn owl,
flew at Rachet to harass; she was a predator. She dipped

low overhead, then flew on as silently as the moonlight. Rachet ducked, then ran forward.

She heard the sound of a wind rushing through a hole. She followed the sound to the stone foundation of the house, found a large break in the wall, and wedged into it. She wiggled along the three-foot-deep crack in the foundation and looked into the basement of the house. She did not jump to the floor but crouched and sniffed.

A strong odor of Queenella was on the air. The boss cat was sleeping in her First Home somewhere in the basement.

Rachet stayed in the break, a passageway created by frost and a settling house. She balanced the possibilities of what to do. Outside were the fox and the owl. Inside was Queenella.

Strewn over the basement were boxes and dried paint buckets, screens, old doors, defunct engines—all manner of discards piled up by people. Then she felt heat—cat luxury. She would dare all obstacles to have a warm home—even Queenella.

Leaping down from the break in the wall to seek

out the heat, she crept between two boxes and under a board leaning against a chest. There she hesitated. Beyond the door was a stack of tires, a paint bucket, and an opening in the junk where there was nothing. Before crossing that space she checked on Queenella. She was sleeping in a box of rags by the hot water pipes. Luxury. Rachet rubbed her own personal scent on the buckets and boxes to make her smell-trail through the junk. To a cat the smell-trail was as bright as neon lights are to people.

Trail announced, she then sought the warmth. It was radiating from the hot air ducts that heated the house. They were warmest near the furnace. She leaped up on the duct and walked toward it.

At a bend where a duct went up into the house, she found a piece of insulation that had been dropped by a workman. The fiber was warm. She lay down. Bliss.

After a few comfortable moments she knew this spot would be her First Home, Queenella or no Queenella. She sprayed her perfume, which said, "This, I will fight for."

5

The heating ducts were as warm as the boy's hands. Rachet lay on her side and spread her toes in the comfort of it. This was better than the boy. He was a human. He was to be avoided. His kind kicked and tortured. She washed off the feeling of the warm hands with her tongue and forepaws, unsheathed her scalpel-like claws, and dozed. She would not be drawn to him.

Many hours later Rachet was awakened by voices coming down the hot air ducts from the large kitchen above her.

"There's a new cat at Roxville Station," said that boy's voice. "She's pretty." Pause.

"Could I have her?"

"No! You know I despise cats." A woman's voice.

"But she'd catch the mice around here."

The woman walked heavily across the floor.

"No. I've told you time and again I don't want any cats in this house." Her voice rose. "I have enough to do, what with all the work to keep you fed and taken care of."

"I would feed her myself. I could use some of the money from my dad's Social Security that I am going to get."

"Cats sneak. They give you the evil eye."

"They're soft and quiet."

"I said I don't like them."

"She'll drive away that ghost you say is in the tower."

"No cats, period. Now, do your chores," she ordered.

The cat argument always ended this way. Alice Dibber, Mike's foster mother, really disliked cats.

Mike rolled up his sleeves and began washing the pile of dishes and pans in the big steel sink. This was one of the chores he had to do for Mrs. Dibber. As he worked, he longed for that spunky Rachet. He remembered how warm the tiger cat had felt in his hands. Somehow she filled an empty space in him. He felt she shared that emotion with him. Rachet, he fantasized, was an orphan, too.

And wonder of wonders, he realized—Rachet was teaching him how to speak "cat."

By watching the Roxville cats and Rachet every day, he was beginning to understand why they held their tails as they did—rank and mood. Why their pupils widened and narrowed—anger and fear when they were wide, and satisfaction when they were narrow. Their ears also talked—back for fear, forward for friendship, and against their heads and down for aggression. But it was mostly their independence that pleased Mike. He admired that.

What is more, he had sensed that Rachet, too, had known a miserable earlier life. Maybe they could make up for it if they had each other.

He wanted her badly. He would figure out how to have her without making Mrs. Dibber mad at him.

When Mr. Dibber died two years ago, Mrs. Dibber was forced to close off the tower and three upstairs bedrooms to save heat. She had moved down to the parlor, where the elegant furniture and the beautifully wrought

Franklin coal stove stood. Mike lived in the upstairs servant's room, impatiently waiting for the four years to pass until he was eighteen and independent . . . like Rachet.

He missed Mr. Dibber. He had been a kindly man and jolly. The two of them had been good friends. They had hung out on the docks together admiring the yachts that were moored there and eating ice-cream cones and hot dogs, which Mrs. Dibber never allowed in the house. They often went out on the sound on Mr. Dibber's boats. He had taught Mike how to keep those boats perfect by caulking, sanding, and painting them. Boats were things of beauty, Mr. Dibber had said, and a path to great adventures.

Mr. Dibber had also taken him to basketball games because he knew Mike liked basketball. Now he was gone. Mike wiped his eyes with his sleeve and thought of Rachet.

He smiled as he rinsed the dishes and pans, thinking what fun he had had with a cat when he was younger. His birth dad had brought home a tabby cat when Mike was seven.

She used to sit on his books while he did his homework, he recalled. To keep her busy and out of trouble, he had put a paper bag on the desk, and in she went. Cats have to go into paper bags, Mike didn't know why. But she would fuss around in it until he got his homework done. She was wonderful.

"Drat," he said out loud to the dishwater, and put a last pan on the old drain board before sweeping the floor. "I want that cat. Well, I'll be eighteen in four years and won't need a foster parent. Then I'll make Rachet my cat." *But I sure would like to have her now,* he thought. *That beautiful, green-eyed tiger cat and me. We're survivors.*

He wiped his hands and ran his fingers through his thick red hair. Mike's square chin jutted forward as he thrust his hands in his blue jeans and walked up the back stairs to his room. That cat, he was thinking, would fill the emptiness in him.

In his room, he wondered if his mother would have let him have a cat. She had been killed in an automobile accident when he was three, and so he would never know. But he wanted to believe that she would have.

Fate had dealt him a dark card. His father had died

five years later, and he had no other relatives. So he had been turned over to the county welfare agencies and offered for adoption. But he was too old and nobody wanted him. Like Rachet.

He had had three pairs of foster parents. One had been a couple in the county-financed group residence and the other a family who kept him for a short while. Then Mike had been turned over to Mr. and Mrs. Dibber. He had been given chores, which he gladly did: dishes, sweeping, garbage, and anything Mr. and Mrs. Dibber asked. The chores helped him find a way into their hearts.

Mrs. Dibber was strict, but he had learned to do what she demanded without protest.

But she had not reciprocated. When he asked for a cat or a turtle, she said a definite no.

When Mr. Dibber passed away, Mrs. Dibber had a hard time taking care of the big house. Hailstones had broken a window in the tower, and Mrs. Dibber was too frugal to have it repaired. So it remained broken. So were some of the shutters. Two years of neglect had earned the house the name "haunted."

Mike tried to like Mrs. Dibber but did wish she would let him keep, if not a cat, a frog or a fish. But she would not.

He stopped dreaming, got his basketball, and left the house. He dribbled it down the sidewalk as he made his way to the home of his friend Lionel Vinski. He passed the house of the bachelor Ernie next door, and the white house that belonged to two sisters, Mame and Janet. He shoveled snow for them every winter and mowed their lawn in summer. The money he earned from this bought him all he needed—magazines, gum, basketball shoes, and notebooks.

At the end of the block in a trim green house surrounded by a rail fence lived Lionel, a husky dark-haired boy who sported the latest high school hairdo this week—gelled green hair.

As always, Mike climbed to the top of Lionel's rail fence and gracefully walked to its end, where he twirled, jumped to the ground, and slam-dunked a basket on the garage. Lionel was outside.

"I like your hair," Mike said, and slammed the ball into the basket again.

"It's supposed to scare you." Lionel laughed, caught the ball, and slam-dunked it.

"Looks good," Mike said ironically. "I wonder what Mrs. D. would say if I went green?"

"She'd eat you for salad." Lionel grinned and slam-dunked another one.

The friends shot baskets until almost dark, when Mike said good-bye and started for home.

A dog barked inside the house.

"What's Stalin doing inside?" he asked Lionel. "I thought he was an outside dog."

"Stalin's mad," Lionel said of the barking dog. "He got away from my dad this morning and almost got a stray cat, but the cat scratched his nose, and you pitched a backpack at Stalin before he could kill it." He laughed.

"Good," Mike said to himself. Out loud he shouted, "Gotta go, it's getting late."

Outside—maybe Rachet . . . He smiled. Could he possibly have Rachet as an outside cat?

Mike jogged to the haunted house, passed Mr. Dibber's abandoned boats on his way to the back door, and started up the steps.

He stopped.

A yellow striped tail disappeared through the hole the frost had made in the foundation.

"Wow! Wouldn't that be something?" he said. "Rachet right here in Mrs. Dibber's house." He smiled. This was better than he had even imagined.

6

Rachet slipped into the basement and wound through the junk to the heating pipes. She was settled comfortably in the environs of Roxville. She had a First Home, a Sunning Spot on the grass near the tire, and a Hunting Lookout in the woods near the bridge where the mice were abundant. She also had a Second Home in case Queenella chased her out of the basement—her tire.

She rarely saw Ringx, the raccoon, on her nightly prowls, for the air had grown colder and had readied her for winter's semihibernation. The crickets had long ago stopped singing. The monarch butterfly was on a pine needle in the mountains north of Mexico City with millions of its kind. Their forest seemed to breathe with the opening and closing of butterfly wings.

In January all the butterflies would turn from "it's" to "he's or she's." They would mate, and then the seemingly fragile butterflies would fly all the way north to the fields and gardens where they had been born.

Meanwhile Shifty, the red fox, was finding rats and mice scarce and wanted to go after wild turkeys. Aware of his intentions, the turkeys roosted in tree limbs, not on the ground. A coyote wandered from his home to the west of town, smelled them, and leaped to reach them. He might have gotten one on the next try had not a train roared into the station and frightened him. He sped to his home territory.

Not until February, a wet, cold month, did Rachet find food getting scarce enough to send her off to the station for the Bent Lady's cat food feast.

One day at the station Rachet came too close to Ice Bucket and spit at her. Ice Bucket, spit back. Rachet hissed and laid back her ears. With that, Ice Bucket drew back, and the battle was over. Rachet moved up another step on the hierarchy ladder. It was a ritual her ancient ancestors had evolved when there were many solitary wild Kaffir cats at the Egyptian granaries. It was their way to ensure food and breeding rights.

At six-thirty in the morning after a mouseless night, Rachet was in the passageway of the stone foundation, waiting for enough time to pass before she followed Queenella to the cat food cans. In the kitchen upstairs, where Mike was getting himself cereal for breakfast, the radio played music, then stopped.

"The day will bring snow and cold as a sprawling zone of low pressure to the northwest joins another zone from the south. This will probably be the storm of the year," said the meteorologist from the National Weather Service. *"The two storms are due to collide over the tristate area.*

"Stock up on batteries and fill your bathtubs with water. We can expect more violent storms like this as the earth warms."

While lying in the passageway waiting to go outside, Rachet saw large flakes falling. More and more fell until the sky was white. Being a cat, she reached out and caught one. It turned to water. She caught more. They, too, melted. Curious and amused, she caught falling snowflakes until Queenella suddenly leaped back inside through the broken glass in the window well. The snow had turned her back from the station. As she reentered she hissed in Rachet's direction. "Mind your rank," she was saying.

Rachet waited until enough time had passed for Queenella to settle herself in the rag box by the hot water pipes. But when she moved to depart, she saw three mice come into the basement through Queenella's broken window. They disappeared in the junk.

Rachet did not have to go to the station; instead she jumped down to the basement floor. The mice had come in out of the storm, and she would have breakfast here.

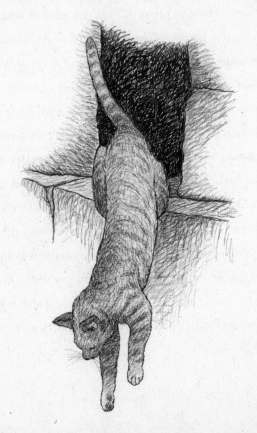

"All schools are closed in the city and the northern suburbs. Snow day. This is a big storm."

"Better get out the snow shovel," said Mrs. Dibber. "I'm going back to bed."

Mike went down to the basement for the shovel and scared a mouse from behind it. Suddenly a cat came out of nowhere and leaped on it. It was Rachet! He silently cheered.

Rachet saw Mike; she remembered his warm hands and let the mouse get away. Still afraid of people, she ran around the chest and off into the shadows of the basement.

"Here, kitty, kitty," Mike called hopefully. He moved a screen, looked behind the chest, but she was a wild cat and did not come to his call; instead she crawled silently into the springs of the broken chair and supported herself on the coils and sat cat-still.

The boy went upstairs and came back with some cooked fish. He sat down on the steps and, holding it out called, "Kitty, kitty, kitty." Rachet didn't move.

"The snow is falling at the rate of several inches an hour in Central Park and more in the northern suburbs."

Mrs. Dibber called to Mike. He went up the steps, taking the smell of fish with him. Rachet dashed toward her First Home on the heating duct. Her whiskers tingled as a faint motion played over them. Ice Bucket! She had left her home to go to the station, only to find herself bogged down in a foot of snow. It was distasteful and cold. She thought of the haunted house, well known to every cat of Roxville, and sped toward it. They knew it by the warmth the old house emanated on winter days and by the scent of Queenella. This was the boss cat's First Home, but in a monster storm Ice Bucket was willing to brave Queenella.

As she went through the familiar hole in the fence, she flipped her paws to rid them of melt. Staggering over the snow, she leaped into the window well and winced. There was more snow there. She dug through it to the broken window and dropped down to the dark basement floor.

Ice Bucket instantly smelled Rachet and Queenella, but that did not turn her away from the warmth. She darted into the coal bin, where the coal was stored for the Frankin stove, and curled up in an overturned bucket. Nervously she placed her feet in springing position, ready to dash off if she had to. But she was relying on cat tolerance to allow her to stay.

Outside a snowplow passed the house and in muted thunder went down the street and across the tracks to the parking lot. Tatters and Tachometer listened to it plow up and down the lot, coming closer and closer as it unfolded walls of snow.

They now felt the unusual pressure of the storm and tensed.

When the snowplow passed the tollbooth, Tachometer ran out. Tatters followed. They took the plowed roadway to the station and sensed that the Bent Lady had not come to feed them. They ran back to the plowed street and headed for the haunted house, a better place than the tollbooth in a bad storm.

At the snowy yard Tachometer slipped under one of the upturned boats and hid on the seat—a hideout she had used before. Tatters, who was just behind her, smelled that Queenella was at home but dove through the window well and into the basement in spite of her. She shook off the snow, maneuvered gracefully among the tires and boxes, and slipped into a partly opened drawer of an old chest.

An hour later Tachometer, still under the boat, felt greater pressure from this major storm and followed Tatters into the basement, Queenella notwithstanding. She found Tatters in the chest, jumped on its top, and then down into the drawer. Rubbing her head against Tatters's head in greeting, she curled beside her.

"This is the blizzard of the year. One hundred thousand people are already without electricity, and there's a pileup on Route 95 a mile long. Use public transportation if you must go out. But remain indoors if you are not needed to fight this storm. Stay tuned to this station for more on the blizzard."

The wind had blown snow through a broken window in the truck where Elizabeth hid. She detested it and headed for the warm, dry haunted house. Entering the house through Rachet's perfumed crack in the foundation, she peered around. She was about to have kittens and had one thing in mind—a nest. Nothing, not even Rachet or Queenella, could stand in the way of that. Finding a barrel of old dresses, she curled up comfortably among sequins and silk. Then she sprayed to tell the other cats that kittens were on the way. They understood her message.

Queenella awoke, smelled the cats, hissed in high decibels, and went back to sleep. They were far enough away in the big basement not to provoke her ire.

Flea Market was the last of the cats of Roxville Station to leave her First Home and come through the snow to the haunted house. She, too, knew of this basement with its warm pipes and heating ducts, and she, too, like all the cats, had felt the pressure of an Arctic storm arriving. Sensibly they all sought the warmth in spite of Queenella. Ice Bucket was in a bucket in the coal bin, Flea Market snuggled in a box of papers, Tatters and Tachometer were in the drawer of a chest, Elizabeth was in the dress barrel, and Rachet was catnapping on her heating duct.

The cats of Roxville were all together in one place for the first time in their lives. The storm blew on.

7

The oil furnace suddenly shut off. The lights went out in the house upstairs, but Roxville Station's feral, independent cats were curled cozily, unaware of light or dark in the basement of the haunted house that belonged to cat-hating Mrs. Dibber.

"All of the northern suburbs are without electricity. There are several feet of snow in Central Park and more falling at the rate of an inch an hour. In some areas—two."

Mike was prepared. He had a flashlight and some candles. He lit an oil lamp and then a coal fire in the Franklin stove. He and Alice Dibber huddled up to it.

"This is where an old house comes in handy," Mrs. Dibber said, holding her hands to the stove. "I'm cold."

"We ought to get a cat. It would warm your lap," Mike said, giving his cat plan another try.

"No."

"It won't cost you a cent," he said, aware of her money consciousness. "I can feed her now that the county officials decided I can have my dad's Social Security money."

"That's not final."

Click, click, click, click, sounded faintly in the heating duct.

"Hear that?" said Mrs. Dibber, sitting forward.

"I did," he said. Curious, he walked to the central heating duct.

"It's the ducts cooling off," said Mike.

"It's that ghost," said Mrs. Dibber.

Mike put his ear against the duct. "Just one cat?" he pleaded.

"No."

"There are few cars and fewer people on the city streets. The snowplows are working against blowing winds and blizzard conditions. They are not keeping up with this storm. Winds are gusting up to forty miles an hour in the city and fifty in the suburbs, where the two storms have met. Temperatures will drop to the single digits during the night."

Mike heated a pot of soup on the top of the Franklin stove and opened a box of crackers. He and Mrs. Dibber ate while they watched the snow pile up to the windowsills, creep up the panes, and cut out the daylight. It was so dark that night seemed to have arrived in midafternoon inside the haunted house.

"I'll get more coal," said Mike, gripping his flashlight and picking up the coal carrier.

Mrs. Dibber wrapped her blue shawl more tightly around her and drew closer to the stove. Mike hurried through the dark kitchen to the basement door. Upon opening it, he was met by a gingery smell. He scanned the basement with his flashlight to find what gave off the odor but saw nothing.

Rachet hissed at Mike from her heating duct. The hiss was above the range of human ears, but Tachometer, Tatters, Ice Bucket, Flea Market, Elizabeth, and Queenella heard it clearly. Rachet had told them that Mike was a potential enemy. They pulled back farther in their buckets and boxes and bureau drawers.

Ice Bucket placed her feet to run as Mike, his coal carrier full, walked right by her.

He was halfway up the steps when he had an over-whelming feeling that the tiger cat was watching him. He shone his light over the basement junk and then to the heating ducts. Rachet's green eyes glowed. Mike's heart thumped.

"Here, kitty, kitty, kitty."

She did not move.

"Cars on Route 95 are snowbound, and most of the city is with-out electricity. The snowplows are having trouble getting through the eight-foot drifts.

"Stay inside. This is a killer blizzard. A house roof in the suburbs has collapsed under the weight of the snow, and there are reports of people trapped in their cars. Let us know where you are. We will get help to you as quickly as we can."

Mike returned to the parlor, added coal to the fire, and tried not to show Mrs. Dibber how pleased he was to have Rachet near. He sat down in the darkness, watching the flames dance in the stove. He was thinking longingly about having Rachet in his lap when there was pounding at the front door. Mike stopped dreaming and hurried to open it. There, red-cheeked and cov-ered with snow, were Lionel Vinski and his parents.

"We saw the smoke from the Franklin stove and

hoped you'd let us in. Can we sleep on your floor by the fire?" Lionel asked. "Our heat and lights are off."

"If you don't have that dog with you," shouted Mrs. Dibber from the parlor.

"I know you don't like Stalin," called Mr. Vinski, "so we left him at home under old coats and a blanket. The house is pitch-black and feels like zero."

"We brought our own food and sleeping bags," called Greta Vinski.

"Come in, come in," answered Mrs. Dibber.

At midnight the parlor floor was strewn with sleeping bodies, and in the basement below them the cats of Roxville hunted mice.

All but one: Elizabeth was making a nest of sorts in the dress barrel between a blue silk gown and a violet shirt—and directly below where Mrs. Dibber was sleeping in the parlor.

Biting off the buttons on the violet shirt and chewing the stays on the blue sequined dress that poked out like sticks, she fashioned a birthing place. Then she washed every part of herself. When she was cat-clean she lay back and purred. Her muscles were contracting and pushing the first kitten from her body.

Slowly at first, then with a rush, the first kitten, a pure black baby except for his white feet, arrived coiled in a membrane. Elizabeth removed it with her tongue and cut with her teeth the umbilical cord through which she had been feeding the kitten for sixty-three days. Then she licked him until he was dry. She stopped and rested, closing her ears to the fifty-mile-per-hour wind gusts.

The kitten's eyes were closed; his ears could not hear the wind and he could not see, but he could smell. His nose led him to his mother's milk. Like iron to a magnet, he wiggled to a teat and grasped it in his mouth. He did not let go until his mother stood up to give birth to a second kitten.

Elizabeth's sixth kitten was born around 5:30 A.M. by her internal clock. An hour later she got to her feet, stretched, and smelled the sweet odor of kittens.

Rachet awoke, inhaled the pheromones from the kittens, and stayed where she was, knowing that Elizabeth would no longer be the shy Elizabeth. She would fight with tooth and claw any animal that came near her kittens: cats, dogs, foxes, even animals as big as humans. Rachet marked a new trail through the basement junk that gave a wide berth to the dress barrel. After making a detour she arrived at her passageway in the foundation.

It was blocked with snow.

She was returning to her heating duct around 8 A.M. when Mike came down the steps to the coal bin. He looked for her in the sweep of his flashlight, calling, "Kitty, kitty, kitty."

Rachet felt something pulling her to him. He had a warm magnetism—but then, he was a human. She hissed hatred in notes too high for him to hear. They described a foot-kicking, torturing human. She arched her back and swished her tail vigorously.

Tachometer heard Mike's "kitty, kitty, kitty" sounds and drew back in the drawer at Rachet's comment. Tachometer had known few humans, having been born in the wilds and raised by a clever feral mother. But Rachet's high hiss was a warning. She crouched in the drawer.

Mike saw Tachometer's ears above the bureau drawer. They were black ears, not yellow.

"There are two cats down here," he said aloud and grinned. "Two cats. Mrs. Dibber would be furious."

Suddenly he heard an explosive screech. It came from the tower ducts, a wild and unhappy scream. It sounded like a movie ghost.

"This house *is* haunted!" he said, and laughed at himself. It had been a high-pitched and lonely screech echoing down the ducts. The wind? The blizzard?

Mike shone his flashlight all around the basement, still looking for Rachet. He couldn't find her, so he slowly went up the stairs to the kitchen. At the sink he glanced out a snowy window at the storm.

The wind had blown the snow into six-foot drifts. The yard and field beyond were Arctic white. Trees were knocked down and buried under igloos of snow. Electric poles were blown over, and their wires were spitting dangerously in the snow.

Mike thought about Rachet and smiled to know she was safe in his house.

At dawn the next day, the deer in the lowland swamp maples made trails to the edible aspens and cedars. They stomped the deep snow to open their avenues to the trees. Their body temperatures were low, a biological maneuver to save energy. The deer came to these lowlands every winter, as had their ancestors before them.

A chickadee on a cedar limb under the snow did not get up at dawn as his internal clock instructed. Instead he remained under the snow cover, where it was warmer than the subzero air above. He chirped. Three other chickadees nearby chirped back.

Shifty, the red fox, had fought off a rival male fox just before the storm by using his brushy tail like a sword. Now he snoozed through the blizzard and its aftermath near his den entrance. He was protecting Shafty, his mate, who would have their pups in April.

In the hollow maple not far from the foxes, Ringx was in partial hibernation, not in the deep hibernation of the groundhogs but in a groggy sleep from which she could awake if she had to.

The turkeys had flown up in the trees to get away from the foxes. There they had puffed up their feathers, for the air between feathers is a far better insulator than wool blankets or parkas. Their bare feet, like all birds' feet, have a circulatory system that allows the feet to cool without cooling the body too much.

Fang had crawled into the chipmunk Cheek's hole

and was curled like a ship's rope in snake-hibernation. Cheeks and his mate were in winter sleep in their bed/ living room.

The mice were tunneling to the seeds under the warmer-than-air snow.

The many animals of Roxville were surviving the blizzard in their ingenious ways.

Mike, on the other hand, was making trips to the coal bin for fuel and looking for Rachet. He smiled when he thought of Mrs. Dibber with beautiful lithe cats living right under her.

8

The power came back on, and the Vinskis went home. They found Stalin sleeping on the couch, where he should not have been. He awoke at their arrival, took one look at their scolding body language, and crept away with his tail between his legs.

The people of Roxville began to shovel out. The first train since the height of the storm pulled into the station around ten o'clock in the morning. It was late because the railroad workers had to thaw the frozen switches and plow the snowdrifts. On the streets of Roxville the emergency vehicles were answering calls for help.

"Many areas are still without power, and the temperature is still below zero. The windchill makes it feel like seventeen below. The county center is open for those who still do not have heat."

Mike went outside and was shoveling the walk when suddenly he wondered if Rachet and the other cats in his basement had enough food. He wasn't worried about water. They would eat the snow. He hurried to finish the walk, then plowed through the snow to the rear of the house. The snow was four feet deep above the stone foundation. No cat could get out to eat snow, much less catch mice. He shoveled furiously, found Rachet's foundation passageway, and dug a path between it and the porch. The cats could jump to it and probably find a mouse among the old shutters and screens there.

Worried that the mice on the porch might not be enough, he dug a path from the porch to the plowed street. He dared not put down cat food for fear Mrs. Dibber would see it and ask questions. With a way to the road cleared, he was satisfied that Rachet and that other cat could get to the station. He hoped the sidewalks around the housing project were cleared so that the Bent Lady could get to the station with her cans of cat food. He did not know about Queenella's window well with the broken window—so he did not dig it out.

Down in the basement Rachet sat on her heating

duct, dozing and waiting patiently for the world to change and the snow to disappear like the rain. She was hungry and thirsty, but she had been hungry and thirsty before. From her past experience she knew that if she moved as little as possible she saved her body fluids and energy. But Queenella had not learned that lesson, and when Mike opened Rachet's passageway Queenella sped with all her cat vigor to claim it.

Seeing her property threatened, Rachet suddenly felt ownership fury. Queenella was on her territory. Despite the fact that Queenella was top cat, Rachet gracefully jumped down from the heating duct. Crouching behind a bucket of dried paint, her haunches high, she got in springing position. This was her domain—her territory. She would defend it. She growled deep in her throat. Queenella heard, stopped, and looked away. Rachet growled again and looked away from Queenella when she looked back.

Rachet tilted her head. Queenella tilted her head, the movement to protect their throats in a fight. Queenella turned her eyes away from Rachet, very aware of her whether she looked at her or not. After long minutes of pretending to ignore each other, they flattened their ears back and down aggressively.

Queenella hissed. She pulled back her lips and uncovered her sharp white canine teeth, a statement to Rachet to take warning. Queenella had made this gesture of battle with her before and won. She was sure the young cat, Rachet, would not challenge her, but to make certain, she growled.

Tachometer and Tatters heard her, peered out of the drawer, then drew in their heads quickly. The gestures of the two cats had told the others that they were ready to fight. Tatters went to the back of the drawer, but Tachometer stayed forward and kept her eyes bravely on the warriors. Her ears cupped forward.

Flea Market jumped up to the heating duct and sniffed the aroma of war. Drawing in her neck to make herself less conspicuous, she watched.

At Queenella's growl, Ice Bucket came out of the coal bin and hunched behind a barrel to watch.

Elizabeth heard nothing. She was busy with motherhood.

Rachet's pupils grew large with anger and fear; her fur bristled. Queenella would not move off her property—her territory.

Queenella smelled Rachet's ire and unsheathed her claws. She smelled of cat war.

Rachet, too, smelled the pheromones of war and pulled in her head to protect her neck, anticipating the worst. She had seen Queenella's unsheathed claws, which spoke of a coming fight.

She looked away, then back when Queenella was looking away. Queenella looked away, then back when Rachet was looking away. A half hour of this and Queenella lifted her hindquarters to dash for the passageway and claim it with her scent.

Rachet sensed this movement on her whiskers and arose. Tail low, she walked stiff-legged toward Queenella, who rolled to her side. Her head and shoulders led her body—a "come fight me" move. Rachet, surprised by this move, stopped walking. Queenella raised a forepaw, feigning a strike. Rachet crept forward again—getting closer.

Queenella struck at Rachet's nose, a sensitive spot on most mammals. Rachet lifted her nostrils out of the reach of her unsheathed claws and breathed lionlike. Queenella swung and missed. Enraged, she grabbed and pulled down Rachet with her forepaws, her mouth open, her voice silent. With her hind feet she tried to claw open Rachet's vulnerable stomach.

Though she was held tightly in Queenella's forepaws and jaws, Rachet's strong rear feet could still rake mercilessly at Queenella's belly. Both cats were on their sides, slashing at each other with claw and tooth. Queenella howled. Rachet hissed, spit, and growled. Suddenly Queenella rolled under Rachet and raked her stomach with her powerful hind feet. Rachet shrieked. Queenella shrieked.

The door to the kitchen opened.

"Who's down there?"

Mrs. Dibber saw the two warring animals from the top of the stairs.

"Cats!" she gasped.

Slamming the door shut, she ran to the phone and dialed the exterminator.

Rachet, alarmed by the appearance of the woman, stopped clawing Queenella's stomach and ran back to her heating duct. Queenella jumped to her feet and without even shaking her ruffled fur, dove through the break in the foundation, spraying her scent on the walls of the passageway to claim it as hers. She jumped out into a snowy world, flipped her paws, and leaped back inside. She sped to her box of rags by the hot water pipes.

Rank changed with that fight. Rachet had battled with

the queen, and they had come off almost even. She was now second in the Roxville cat hierarchy.

After the fight Queenella did not pay any attention to Rachet, and Rachet did not pay any attention to Queenella. They knew their positions, and by obeying them the cat rule of tolerance was established.

The other cats reacted to the fight by washing vigorously. Then they went back to sleep as if nothing had happened.

Rachet growled. For now she stayed on the duct. But she must have that rag box by the hot water pipes. It was so cozy, but mainly it was a sign of supremacy—Queenella's First Home.

9

The phone rang in the Boot It Pest Exterminator office; the owner answered it.

"Yes—you what?" He loosened the bandanna around his neck with his thumb and ran his hand through his thinning hair.

"Lady, I'm up to my ears busy. The mice and rats have come out of the storm and into so many basements I can't count them.

"What, you want to get rid of cats, not rats? Lady, you'd better call the SPCA.

"You what? Want them killed?

"They're feral cats? How do you know?

"Lady, I'm in your area this morning, and I'll take a look and see what I can do."

Mrs. Dibber hung up the phone as Mike came in

from the fort he and Lionel were building in the back-yard. She sat down at the kitchen table and folded her arms.

"I called the exterminator," she said. "There are cats in my basement." She arose stiffly but with authority and asked Mike if the front walk was cleared. She didn't wait for an answer but said, "The exterminator will be here soon. He can't get to the front door with all that snow."

"Rachet," Mike breathed. He had to think quickly. He decided not to tell her he had already cleared the walk. He would go out the front door and make her think he was outside to shovel snow while he was really in the basement shooing away the cats. He didn't have much time.

"Oh, okay," he said to her, as if reluctant. "I'll get Lionel to help me and make the work go faster." Knowing that Lionel had gone home for lunch, Mike hurriedly put on his coat and walked out the front door, scraped his snow shovel noisily on the porch, then plodded around to the old chute that rolled the coal for the stove down into the bin. He dug it free of snow, opened it, and took off his coat. Feet first, he slid down into the gloomy bin. Ice Bucket hissed in decibels above human hearing.

By the time Mike's eyes had adjusted to the darkness he heard the exterminator at the top of the steps.

Pulling an old tarp over himself, he crouched down.

"Cats," he heard Mrs. Dibber say from the top of the steps.

"I hate cats, too," the exterminator answered. "I'm a dog person myself."

The man turned on his flashlight, came down the steps, and stood not four feet from Mike. Rachet watched from the heating duct, her feet under her, ready to run.

The man set a big canister on the floor while he measured the basement to figure how much fumigant he needed. He flashed his light over the basement, and two pairs of green eyes shone on the heating duct. Mike hissed, catlike, to divert him. The exterminator turned toward Mike to locate the sound and Rachet looked away.

As Mike watched from a hole in the tarp, he wondered how he could get out before the fumigant overpowered him. Just then the exterminator saw the broken window and yelled up to Mrs. Dibber that the fumigant would escape through it.

"Can't have that," he said, walking over to the window and measuring the pane.

Then the exterminator went up the cellar steps to the kitchen to tell Mrs. Dibber he was going to get glass for the window.

"I sure hate cats," he said, realizing he had an ally in Mrs. Dibber. "I'll be back later and we'll get them cats. Good riddance.

"Cats," he grumped, and went through the foyer and out the front door, leaving the canister on the basement floor.

After he was gone Mike rubbed his hands and clothes all over the coal chute before he shinnied up and into the snow. He hoped that Rachet would follow his scent and leap up and out to safety. A cat can smell a human's worry scent, he had learned.

Rachet sprayed an alarm when she smelled the aroma from the canister and left the basement through her hole. The other cats smelled the odor of fear in her spray. It was a cat siren. Ice Bucket ran out of the coal bin and dove through the foundation passageway.

She hesitated in the cold, then took Mike's path through the snow to the porch. Gracefully she leaped up to it and hid among the deteriorating screens and shutters. Tachometer smelled the alarm, leaped out of the drawer, crossed the open space, and went out through Queenella's window. She found Ice Bucket's trail, followed it, and leaped to the porch but did not join her. Instead she continued on around to the front steps and down into the plowed street. Keeping low, she slunk back to the parking lot, avoiding people by hesitant runs and stops. The plow had cleared the way to the tollbooth, and she dove into her First Home and disappeared in the supports.

Tatters was out of the basement behind Tachometer and followed her sister's scent to the tollbooth. She rubbed her head against Tachometer's head in greeting and lay down beside her.

Flea Market smelled the fear on the air and set out in a panic for the passageway. It reeked of Queenella. With the alarm odor still burning her nose, she stole along the wall and dove through Queenella's forbidden window, a brave exit for Flea Market.

Once outside she smelled that Tachometer and Tatters and Ice Bucket had jumped to the porch. She jumped, too, ignored Ice Bucket behind the shutters and screens, and flowed smoothly down the front steps and out into the street. Tail down, back straight, she hurried to an open Dumpster. Inside she found some shredded papers and curled up on them.

Queenella had left the basement when she first heard the man's harsh voice upstairs. She took the plowed sidewalk to Mame and Janet's house and crawled under their porch.

Elizabeth was the only cat left in the basement. Chemicals of fear and fumigants notwithstanding, she would not leave her six blind and helpless kittens. She covered them with her body to protect them from disaster and remained with them all night.

Then a tick that had gorged itself after biting the hairless interior of her ear let go and fell beside her paw. It crept along, fat and turgid, hunting for a place to lay eggs.

Upon seeing the tick, Elizabeth became desperate to move her kittens. Vermin were worse than fears of a dog to a mother cat. She could claw at a dog's nose but could not crush the life from something so tough and small as a tick. Clutching a kitten by the scruff of the neck, she carried it out Queenella's window into the cold and snow. She smelled Ice Bucket and followed her odor to the porch. Ice Bucket was in the center of the stacked screens, warm and cozy. Elizabeth put the kitten down as far from Ice Bucket as she could, but sheltered by a broken shutter and right under Mrs. Dibber's nose, so to speak.

With a rolling murmur to the kitten to stay put, she went back for another. Meanwhile Mr. Boot It Pest Exterminator had returned with his son to fix the window.

"We'll fumigate as soon as we put this window back," the exterminator said to his son. Afraid of them as she was, Elizabeth determinedly carried a third kitten to the porch. It was her last trip. He fixed the window and then said to his son, "I'm ready to release. Go tell the lady and the boy to leave now, Buster."

Buster clumped up the steps to the kitchen, stuck his head through the door, and shouted to Mrs. Dibber that it was time for them to leave.

Mike picked up Mrs. Dibber's leather suitcase and his own backpack and went out the back door. Something flew overhead, and he looked up to see a large white figure swirl around the tower and vanish.

Suddenly he blinked. "Must be Mrs. Dibber's ghost," he laughed. Just then, he saw a small yellow-colored cat on a limb of the maple tree. Relief flooded through him. In that moment he went from worry to joy.

"Rachet," he whispered. "You're safe." He hoped the other cat was safe, too.

Happy now, he went on to the Vinskis' house, kicked the snow off the fence rail, and balancing suitcase with backpack, he danced along it to the Vinskis' front side-walk. Whooping, he jumped down, tangoed up the walk, and knocked on the door. Lionel opened it, saying Mrs. Dibber was already there.

Minutes later the fumigant filled the basement. It seeped under the doors and into the kitchen and parlor of the Victorian house. There it thinned out and cleared.

The next day Mike and Mrs. Dibber returned home. Mr. Boot It Pest Exterminator came and later reported that he had found three dead kittens—and that was it. No big cats at all. But he collected his fee and carried off the kittens to dump in his refuse can. He wondered only briefly what had happened to the cats Mrs. Dibber had seen.

Mike watched him go with relief and cheered the wily Rachet's escape to the maple tree. She must have sensed something evil. He wondered how.

"If cats have nine lives," he mused, "then Rachet has ten or fifteen."

Rachet stayed on the maple limb, cat-patient. That night she came down from the tree and wound her way to her tire. She dug down to it. After the fumigation she never returned to the basement of the haunted house.

10

The thaw came suddenly. Warm winds blew up from the south and the temperature rose to sixty—unseasonable for March.

In the warm air the snow melted rapidly, flooding the river and streams. Paper cups and newspapers washed to the drainage outlets and blocked them, flooding the sidewalks and streets.

Thousands of starlings blackened the sky as they responded to the unusually warm weather by leaving their winter roosts in the city and flying north to Roxville. The sunlight still read winter, and they upended on wing and flew back.

Half asleep, Rachet listened to a male red-winged blackbird creak his "rusty pump" songs from the reeds that edged the Olga River. Dozens of golden-crowned kinglets in the treetops sang in choir. If the warm weather persisted, they would head north to the tall forest treetops where they build their hanging nests, but if the cold returned, they would fly south or starve. The weather was strange this year and mixed up some of the birds who respond to high and low temperatures.

A Carolina wren that had lived all the winter in the deer lowlands flew to a tree near Rachet to glean the insects that came awake on warm days. After eating and singing a bubbling song, he went back to the upturned tree roots by the river where his mate was busy. She was so confused by the weather that she had carried sticks to start a nest in a cozy cave in the roots a few months early.

Very much responding to the warmth, too, the male sang forty of his forty-one songs to notify his neighbor Carolina wren that this land was his. His neighbor sang back. To mark their territory, birds sing at each other instead of fighting.

Mike went to school earlier than usual by way of the station to look for Rachet. When he arrived, she was eating at one of the cans of cat food. He was so pleased that he gave a thumbs-up.

Rachet lifted her head and looked at him, then looked away. He wondered what she was doing. The movement was so balletlike that he imitated her in fun. He looked away when she looked at him. He looked back when she looked away. And strangely he felt as if he were bonding with her.

Rachet for her part sensed that here was a human who talked "cat." She purred.

During the following month of April, Mike was able to move within six feet of Rachet, then five, then four.

"She likes me," he said out loud excitedly. But when he reached out to pet her, she ran, and he added to himself, *in her mysterious way.*

11

Wary of the haunted house, Rachet took up a First Home in a large green briar bush at the edge of the woods amid sumac, maple saplings, and thorns. She scratched out a winding tunnel through the bush to some sticks and leaves and settled down there. Not even Shifty could get past the briars to get to her, and Mr. Vinski now kept Stalin on a heavier leash. The rain did not get through the dense stems, and she was safe and dry.

Even though she had a new home, Rachet still thought about the box of rags by the hot water pipes. If she could claim it she would remove Queenella from her top position in the order of the cats of Roxville Station. She, Rachet, would reign.

She contracted and opened her claws in pleasure at the thought of the food and of the First Home that being top cat would assure her.

The days went from warm to cold several times and then it was May. The Roxville wildlife really became busy. Starlings were building nests, Shifty and Ringx were nursing pups, and Windy was feeding half-grown owlets. She caught them mice by listening to the sounds the animals made, rather than by seeing them. One ear is lower than the other in all owls so that they can triangulate on rustles and movements. Once a sound is pinpointed, they zero in on the prey on a sound crossbar and strike it without seeing.

One night after swooping up a mouse just that way at the Olga River cliffs, Windy flew with it to her owlets, "hearing" the many limbs of the woods without touching one. Her hearing was that precise and accurate.

She swept low over the green briar tangle, heard Rachet breathing, and veered out over the field to her owlets.

At daybreak Rachet heard Stalin sniffing her trail, then felt the scraping of his dragging leash coming closer and closer. He was loose. Running hard behind him came Mr. Vinski, and in no time they were at her thicket entrance. Mr. Vinski grabbed Stalin, who barked to announce Rachet's presence, but Rachet was high in the briar bush.

Stalin kept barking until Mr. Vinski hauled him back to the bicycle path. Rachet hissed.

Confused by the warm weather, a female cardinal laid a stick in a shrub fork and started a nest. When she built a nest, her mate didn't help but sang clearly and loudly that she was his and this was his territory. He would feed her sweet tidbits after it was finished and she was ready to lay eggs. But that would be almost a month from now. This warm and cold weather had mixed up the cardinals as well as the Carolina wrens.

The birds flew off. Sensing only deer in the woods, not fox or owl, Rachet rolled on her back, legs outstretched, and yawned. The deer and her yearling walked right by Rachet. The doe was teaching her fawn her secret path to the best food. She led him to a garden of hostas. They ate them all and casually vanished into the morning shadows. The deer had yarded in the lowlands all winter where they could eat only cedars and twigs. They were now enjoying the sweet young plants in the gardens and yards of the suburbs.

Two house sparrows nested early. By the end of May they had already built a nest in the eaves of the tollbooth and laid six eggs. When they hatched, Tachometer heard the peeping young and jumped up on the roof. She pussyfooted toward the eaves from which the noise came. Suddenly she slid on the tin. Though she dug in her claws, she skated down the roof and off. She landed on all fours on the asphalt below and tried again. Again she slipped and wisely gave up.

Tachometer heard the sparrow babies, but last year's roof accidents had taught her she could not walk on tin. So she waited. In about a week one ambitious baby bird fluttered to the ground. Tachometer went after it. Suddenly a car drove between them, and when it had passed, the bird was gone.

The other nestlings stayed in the nest until they could fly. Tatters and Tachometer watched them wing overhead.

So did Mike, who was now interested in all cat behavior because of Rachet. He had been following Tachometer and Tatters to find out where their First Home was. He had observed that cats avoid other cats, and he wondered why these two liked each other. They were the same size and marked somewhat alike. He decided they must be littermates like his teacher's two friendly cats. They played and slept together, she said. And so did Tatters and Tachometer.

The two were behind the tollbooth when the sparrow nestlings suddenly fledged. Tatters swung a paw, Tachometer jumped for them, and Mike made a note of the fact that they hunted together.

June filled the field and air with young mice, rats, birds, and voles. The cats of Roxville Station lived well.

Elizabeth, however, was not a good hunter. She was teaching her three kittens to depend upon the kindness of the Bent Lady for food. Mike was learning that cats are individuals—some are good hunters, some poor, and others, like Rachet, are bold.

One morning when Mike was waiting at the station for Rachet, he saw Ice Bucket fighting for a higher rank. The dirty white cat was old enough to test her rank. She walked up to and hissed at Flea Market, the third-ranking cat. Ice Bucket raised her fur to make herself look bigger than she was. Flea Market hissed and tilted her head. Ice Bucket arched her back and spit. They batted paws, claws unsheathed. Flea Market ran under the station platform. With those innocent-looking gestures, Ice Bucket was now third-ranking cat and said so by holding her tail almost as high as Queen-ella's. Rachet, who was second-ranking cat, saw Ice Bucket's new rank by the height of her tail. Ranks were changing, as they do among house cats and people.

By the time school was almost out, Rachet had dared to come within two feet of Mike before she ran. Then one sunny morning she almost touched him, her ears and tail up to say she felt comfortable in his presence.

"Meow," she suddenly said.

It was the "meow" cats give only to humans. Surprised at herself, she arched her back and sped off. But Mike had heard friendliness in her "meow" and smiled.

"I am her person," he said.

Rachet ran all the way back to her briar bush and was settling down, with mixed feelings about Mike, when the ground moved beneath her. She lifted her paw as all around her large insects dug out of the soil. She sniffed them. Big-eyed but blind, they climbed up a stem of the briar bush and stopped. Slowly they split their nymphal coats. When they stepped out of these shells, they were not drab nymphs anymore but colorful adult cicadas.

They had been in the ground for seventeen years eating roots—seventeen years! Rachet was not interested in eating them, but Lysol, the striped skunk, was. She gobbled as many as she could and carried others back to her young, who were denned in the old groundhog burrow. She would begin their hunting lessons with cicadas.

For weeks hundred of thousands of cicadas emerged. Rachet stepped around them, batted them, and played with them; Lysol ate furiously. Lysol's young-sters learned that the red-eyed insects, with their trans-lucent wings and lazy flight, were delicious and easy to catch, but this was hardly a lesson they would benefit from. No wild skunk lived for seventeen years.

The cicadas would sing, mate, and lay eggs. The adults would then die, but their eggs would hatch and live underground for seventeen more years.

One morning, Mike was at the station looking for Rachet when a crew of railroad workers arrived and be-gan tearing up the platform. He asked the foreman what they were doing. The foreman explained that they were going to change over to electric trains instead of diesel and build an entirely new station. He said that a third rail carrying the electricity was going to be laid and that the rail was extremely dangerous. So that no one would get hurt by the electric rail, they were putting up a high fence on either side of the railroad. Mike listened, wondered what Rachet and her associates would do, but didn't have time to tell him about the cats of Roxville Station. He was almost late for school.

The Bent Lady arrived at the station late that morning. The cats of Roxville Station came running from truck, tollbooth, field, and haunted house.

"This is the last time you can feed those cats," the foreman said to her. "The health department will take care of them from now on."

The Bent Lady put down her cans and stared at him. "What do you mean?"

"I mean the health department will take care of them." The tone of his voice was ominous. She backed slowly away.

The foreman turned to a man on his crew.

"Feral cats are a nuisance," he said. "Get out the meat with the poison in it."

The Bent Lady heard and was horrified. Poison! She went down the southbound steps at a clip that astonished the foreman and hurried home.

12

In the shadows of that evening's dusk, the Bent Lady left her small apartment in the housing project and went to the station. She stepped off the platform onto the tracks and flashed her light around, looking for the poisoned food. At the spot where she fed the cats she found four chunks of poisoned meat, put them in a plastic bag, and looked for more. The next train was due in half an hour, so she lingered on the tracks, searching.

It was almost train time when she picked up two more pieces. Hurriedly stepping back up on the platform, she missed one piece of meat. The Bent Lady had planned to dump the tainted meat in the station Dumpster, thought better of it, and walked all the way to the main street of town to put the bag in a Dumpster behind a grocery store. She didn't want those railroad workers to find it.

She walked back, crossed over the tracks, and passed the tollbooth where Tatters and Tachometer were just starting out to hunt mice. She did not see them.

Pleased with her accomplishment but saddened almost to tears by the thought she could never feed her cats again, she opened her door and went in. At her kitchen table she put her head in her hands.

"How can they take my cats away from me? What will I do?"

Early the next day Mike went to the station and looked for Rachet. She wasn't there, nor were the other cats or the Bent Lady. Worried, he sat down on a crate and waited until the railroad workers arrived and began laying that third rail—an electric rail that would power the new trains.

The foreman walked over to Mike.

"Enough electricity will run through the third rail," he warned, "to kill a man instantly.

"We're putting fences around the stations to protect people," he said. "There's a crew hanging DANGER. HIGH VOLTAGE signs right now."

The foreman paused to catch a breath. "There will be new steps, an elevator to a new walkover, as well as steps down to a platform for the city-bound trains."

Mike wondered what would become of the cats.

"You can't wander around here anymore," the foreman said firmly. "That's an order." He put his hand
on Mike's shoulder and pointed him toward the platform exit.

Over the next several weeks the old Roxville Station
platform was pulled apart and new cement was poured.
Workmen erected a covered walkway and stairs over the
dangerous tracks.

All this construction caused many rats to run from
the platform's foundation into town. Chirping house
sparrows flew out of the eaves, abandoning the homes
where they had raised young and roosted for genera-
tions. After fluttering from building to building and
chirping loudly, they settled down in the gables and
rainspouts of the houses and stores around Roxville.

But at the station no cats appeared.

From the field Mike watched the workers and worried about Ratchet and the others. Where were they?
He had seen some signs of them—half-buried feces, a
bird's feathers—but no cats. He knew by now that these

feral cats were clever. They were somewhere, and he was determined to find them. Rachet in particular.

When the fence was finished, Tachometer and Tatters were cut off from the other cats of Roxville Station. Being resourceful, they simply went off to find the many mice in other places. They parted company forever, feeling no remorse. Cats walk alone.

Tachometer found a temporary home under the raspberry bushes in the deer lowlands. Tatters settled down under a Dumpster in the housing project. At night she stalked the mice.

Ice Bucket, not being able to get to her TV crate for all the machinery parked around it, wandered up the bicycle path and found shelter under a thorny multiflora rosebush. It was near a trash can settled by mice.

Flea Market, her avenues and highways disrupted by the workmen, went to a jungle of vines she knew. They were just off the bicycle path. A week later she was hunting voles when a jogger saw her and stopped running.

"Aww, a kitty," she murmured, her heart going out to Flea Market.

"Kitty, kitty, kitty," she called in a high, sweet voice. It was a sound humans have learned over thousands of years to attract house cats. Flea Market heard its insistent magic, sat down, sphinxlike, and turned her bright golden eyes on the girl.

The girl inched toward her.

"Kitty, kitty," she repeated over and over again.

Flea Market did not run. She felt the domestic cat in herself and came toward the girl. She meowed. With that, the girl reached out and picked her up, a ragged but charming tabby. She wrapped the cat in a sweater, hugged her, then carried the cat quickly to her car. Flea Market did not fight. The darkness of the sweater had calmed her. The girl put her on the front seat and drove off. The once feral cat lay still.

"Kitty," the girl said as she turned into the driveway of a splendid house, "you have a home."

Several evenings later the Bent Lady, sitting at her window in the housing project, saw Tatters jump off the neighbor's windowsill and melt into the dusk. She hurriedly got to her feet, opened a can of cat food, and put it on her doorstep.

Two hours passed. The sun went down, and in the long shadows the Bent Lady saw Tatters eating from the can. She clapped her hands together and smiled.

Tachometer, sensing the Bent Lady's food from as far away as the deer lowlands, came to the housing project. After eating she made a First Home in the rafters of the furnace room near the Bent Lady's doorstep. She rolled on her back to rub scent on the rafter, and then rubbed it with her cheeks and lips. She had a First Home. She could only go in and out when the door was left ajar, as it often was in warm weather. It would do until late autumn.

Elizabeth seemed not to care that she was visible to the people on the bridge as she walked along the river's edge. Her pupils were large and her tail, usually held low, was now wedged between her legs. She wobbled as she walked. Something was wrong.

Elizabeth was ill from that piece of poisoned meat. She turned away from the river, stumbled into the wood ferns along the edge of the forest, and slept forever.

Elizabeth had given her three kittens to the Roxville wild lands. One was a tomcat that Mike named "Read," because he was all black and white like a letter. The other two were "Triborough," a calico, and "Rumpus," another black-and-white cat. Read went off to the country and found himself a cat city there. Triborough and Rumpus were picked up by a man in the neighborhood and taken to a cat adoption center.

Volton, the tomcat, returned. All the cats of Roxville Station were aware of him through their whiskers, noses, and ears. Volton left the river to prowl the field, caterwauling his mating cry as he searched his Roxville

territory for Queenella. He didn't find her, but he did find Rachet.

For three nights he called to her with his eerie screams. It was summer when Volton departed from Roxville to visit his family of cats in the farming country—and Rachet was pregnant. She purred.

Mike no longer came to the train station. When he was not doing chores or shooting baskets with Lionel he was looking for Rachet. He thought she must be somewhere near his house, now that she was fenced off from the tracks and the station was booming with workmen and machines.

Rachet smelled the intensity of Mike's oak-leaf scent and knew the boy was seeking her. She was wary of him and yet felt drawn to him. Not knowing why, she moved her Sunning Spot to a pile of discarded roof shingles in the field near the haunted house. She did and didn't want to see the boy. She still had a First Home under the briar bush near the river.

One morning Mike walked the rail fence as usual on his way to shoot baskets with Lionel. When he arrived at the Vinski house, Lionel was still in bed. Waiting for him to get up, Mike shot baskets in the driveway. But he had a sense of being watched. For some intuitive reason he glanced at the shingle pile in the field and saw Rachet's orange-striped fur against the dark wood.

"Rachet," he said out loud to her. "There you are! I'm so glad to see you."

To himself he said, *I might win her out of the wild if I can get money for cat food.*

He tossed the ball at the basket and missed, wonder-

ing how to get money and also be outdoors this summer—with Rachet.

I'll plant a garden in the backyard and sell the crops, he said to
himself. *You have to be outdoors a lot with a garden.* Then he
thought, *No, the deer would eat it.*

When Lionel appeared they shot baskets for almost
an hour. Then Mike took the backyard trail home,
jumping fences as he went. In his own yard he glanced
at Mr. Dibber's abandoned boats. Idea! He ran up the
steps and into the kitchen, where Mrs. Dibber was sitting in her bathrobe watching TV, her gray hair still
up in rollers.

"You know, Mrs. Dibber," he said, trying to sound
casual, "I could fix up those old boats of Mr. Dibber's
this summer, and we could sell them for a good price at
the boat docks."

Mrs. Dibber stopped watching TV and turned around
in her chair. She looked at him pleasantly.

"Mr. Vinski keeps asking what I am going to do with
those boats," she said. "He says they are unsightly. I've
been telling him I'm sentimental about them." She
pinched her eyebrows together. "But if you fixed them
up and we sold them . . ."

"I could fix them up like new. Mr. Dibber taught me
how," Mike said. "And we could make some money,"
he added.

"Well, maybe we should do that," said Mrs. Dibber,
and she ran her fingers over her chin. "I'll think about
it tonight," she said and sighed. "I'm sentimental about
those boats."

The next morning she told Mike that she was agree-
able to his plan, and wanted to know when he would
start.

"Now," he said, and gleefully headed downtown to
the hardware store for marine paint, caulking material,
and sandpaper.

"You got money?" the store owner asked.

"Mrs. Dibber has money," Mike answered. "She's
very frugal."

"Frugal!" the store owner humphed. "That's putting
it nicely."

But he let Mike have the materials on credit and take
the purchases home. Mike told him he was fixing up
Mr. Dibber's old boats to sell and would certainly earn
enough cash to pay back the debt.

Mike started work on the white boat that was in the corner of the yard. It was nearest the field with the pile of shingles where Rachet sunned. When he pulled the blue tarp off the boat, Ice Bucket jumped down from the bow seat and ran into the field. She had been hunting house mice from under the cover of the boat. There were mice all over the yard. At forty days of age a mouse is old enough to mate, and in twenty more days it gives birth to ten or twelve babies. It no sooner gives birth than it mates again and in twenty days, when the first litter is on its own, has ten or twelve more babies. Meanwhile the ten or twelve first mouselings are old enough to mate and give birth to ten or twelve more each. That's a lot of mice. Ice Bucket was eating well.

Ice Bucket ran from Mike through the fence hole and into the field.

One night Rachet went out to hunt young rabbits with her tail lifted in the "I am pursuing a rabbit" position and her chest low to the ground. She was gliding toward the wild millet patch where rabbits fed—closer to the yard where Mike worked. He was frequently outside with his boats during the day.

It was full summer. The ragweeds were half grown and the staghorn sumacs were morphing from flower to seeds. Through these smells Rachet stalked the herbal odor of rabbit. Curling her whiskers forward, and smelling with her nose, she sensed a rabbit in the haunted-house yard. She leaped through the hole in the fence, using her night vision, and hid under the boat that Mike had been working on. A moment later it sprinkled, then showered. She waited until the rain was over for the cottontail to appear. It did not. Rachet remained on the bottom of the oarsman's seat.

It showered off and on all night.

The sprinkles finally stopped in the morning. Mike burst out the door, jumped down the steps two at a time, and stood by the upside-down boat.

Rachet found herself looking at his left leg. She suddenly had an overwhelming desire to rub it with the scent glands on her sides and claim him as her property.

She hesitated. She was scared. Suddenly she rubbed her head against Mike's leg. Next she rubbed her cheek against him and then the full length of her lithe body. This human being was hers. They smelled alike now. Mike's hand came down slowly. He stroked her head. She did not hiss but rather cupped her ears forward. Her face smoothed out.

"Meow."

"Rachet, you like me!" He got down on his knees to take her in his arms. With a clatter, he dropped the caulking material he was using. It alarmed Rachet. She ran. She made friends on her terms, not his. The yellow-and-orange-colored cat had leaped through the hole in the fence and disappeared.

"Rachet," he called, and ran to the fence to look for her in the field.

But she was in the tire.

That night she gave birth to five tiny kittens.

13

At dawn Rachet rolled to her side so that each blind and deaf kitten could find a teat, suckle her milk, and begin growing toward a membership in the club of feral cats. When all five were nursing, she put her head down and rested.

This was Rachet's life for almost a week. Then one day her kitten Coal Tar, the firstborn, black kitten with white paws, woke her with a high, sharp "miaow" from outside the tire. Coal Tar had wobbled into the grass and was calling, "Come save me. I am lost." He was too young to generate heat for his body, so he was unable to keep warm without his mother.

"Miaow."

Rachet raced to him, picked him up by the scruff of the neck, which automatically caused him to curl his feet in the fetal position, and carried him back to the nest. She dropped him hard as discipline, then lovingly curled around the kitten to warm and feed him.

Coal Tar suckled, and as the warm milk flowed into him he purred. It is a sound only given when a cat is in the presence of a living thing—a bug, a butterfly, or a human.

Rachet had become a social animal. She was no longer a loner. A mother with five kittens, she was a member of a tight group in which each depended upon the other. Rachet nursed the kittens, cleaned them, and kept them warm. They took the milk she gave and stimulated her to make more milk. Later she would teach them to hunt and educate them in the lay of the land and animals.

When the kittens were ten days old, their eyes and ears opened and they could keep warm by themselves. Now Rachet could leave them for longer periods, but if getting her own food took too long, she returned without having eaten.

At three weeks old their hunting lessons began. The first step was to bring the kittens a dead mouse. They batted it around and chattered their teeth with cat pleasure. The next step was to teach them to roll in its scent until they knew a mouse well. Then she brought home a live, stunned-but-not-killed mouse. Coal Tar jumped on it immediately. It got away, and a sister jumped on it. Rachet's claws had stimulated some anesthesia to flow in the prey, and the mouse felt no pain. It was dead but also alive.

The kittens jumped on the mouse, gaining more and more skill as they played—and then they let it go.

Rachet came home one night in the predawn light to find that a doe and her fawn had eaten and were now trampling the protective goldenrod around her tire. She spat at them and unsheathed her claws. They looked at her curiously, then calmly walked off, but it was too late. The plants were crushed and no longer covered the strong odor of sweet, milky kittens.

A tomcat that had sneaked into Volton's territory while he was away, smelled the sweet kittens, and was tracking them down. He, like all male cats, would eat another male's offspring to be sure only his own offspring survived, but also to make the mother ready to mate soon again.

Rachet checked on her brood. They were all there.

She could not count, but she knew the feeling of five kittens. Suddenly she smelled the tomcat's peppery pheromones close by. She sped out of the tire and stood on the broken goldenrod, arched her back, and spit, ready to attack. The tomcat smelled her motherly ire and pulled back.

Coal Tar was clinging to a teat when his mother left the tire in such haste. He let go and fell in the trampled plants—and the tomcat leaped for him. Rachet pressed back her ears, uncovered her sharp teeth, and dove for the tomcat's neck. She missed. He turned and raced down the fox trail. Minutes later he growled from a limb of the maple.

Rachet grabbed Coal Tar by the scruff of the neck and raced away. She must move her kittens. A tomcat was after them. She ran—not to the briar-bush thicket, not to the rocks by the river, but to her enemy—people. She sped right for the basement of the haunted house.

Despite all her independence, she sought humans. It was not for their handouts of food. It was not even for their shelter. It was for that mysterious bond that exists between cats and humans. Over the ages, cats and humans have developed a warm and loving relationship. It had begun with the cultivation of grain, which brought the small wild Kaffir cat out of the Sahara Desert to catch the mice and rats around the granaries. Once there, they charmed the Egyptians into permitting the cats to come in their houses and sleep on their beds and pillows. They also trained them to catch fish and birds.

The Kaffir cat was so talented and beautiful that the Egyptians proclaimed her a goddess and named her the Goddess Bast.

Something happened around 2000 B.C. The wild Kaffir cats developed smaller heads, shorter legs, and evolved into a new species—a domestic animal. They were like domestic sheep, cattle, and dogs, but not quite like them. The domestic cat could still live in the wild—without man.

Nevertheless the new and domesticated cat, *Felis catus* (its Latin or scientific name), was welcomed for its beauty and skills. But humans soon learned that this friendship was only on the cat's own terms. The cat remained independent. It could live entirely on its own in the wilds or sit on a satin pillow and be fed. Rachet, despite her wretched early treatment by humans, felt that ancient bond and so carried her kitten away from the tomcat, toward the boy.

As she approached the haunted house, a bat family flew out of the tower, sweeping the skies with their wings and catching mosquitoes and moths. They dove low over Rachet, who had disturbed a colony of flying ants, and scooped the insects into their tails.

Without a pause for bat or ant, Rachet leaped up into the overturned boat and climbed to the bow. The wooden cover on the bow, now upside down, made a floor that was a perfect nest for kittens. Into it she tucked Coal Tar, growled softly to tell him to stay put, and went back for a second kitten.

The tomcat's odor was on the tire when she came back—and two kittens were gone. Racing against time and the tomcat, she ran to the boat with the two remaining kittens and lowered her body over the three. Coal Tar sensed the danger and "miaowed."

It was still night when she finally nestled the kittens to her breast. She purred, the kittens purred. A firefly in the grass below turned on its light and walked up to the top of a stalk while the kittens watched him. Once there he spread his two gossamer and two hard chitin wings and took off. High in the trees, he flashed his light twice to the females in the grass, "Are you ready?" One answered "yes" with a single flash, and the firefly flew down to her. Rachet and the kittens watched until his cold light—the mystery of the fireflies—went out. Then the kittens rolled and tumbled in play until they fell asleep at dawn.

Rachet listened with her sensitive ears for the tomcat but heard only the leafhoppers and katydids.

During the summer, Mike tried to get up early so that he would be out of the house before Mrs. Dibber came down to the kitchen. She was always giving him grief about how long the boat restoration project was taking. He didn't want her to discover that he spent time looking for a beautiful yellow-and-orange cat with green eyes.

This morning when he went down to the kitchen, he found Mrs. Dibber also up early and scrambling eggs.

"There you are," she said.

"Yes, ma'am," he replied. "I got up early to work on the boat."

"Mr. Dibber would have had it done and sold by now," she complained.

"It's harder than you think," he apologized. "I want to make it real good, like Mr. Dibber taught me. That way, we'll make more money."

"Nonsense," she said. "I saw you by the Olga River with that basketball idler, the Vinski boy. What were you doing there?"

Mike sighed. How on earth had she seen him?

"I wasn't with Lionel," he said. "I was helping Ron look for a barn owl nest. He's from the Audubon Society. He says there's a barn owl nest somewhere near here and he wants to find it. He's writing a book or something."

"What does he want to find?"

"A barn owl. He found a casting near here, a pellet of fur and bones that owls don't digest and cast up. Isn't that cool? He wondered if I had seen where the owl nested, and I was taking him to the cliffs on the Olga River. I have seen some big owls there."

"Well, that's silly," she huffed. "A grown man like that, too. Looking for owls. Now you get back to that boat and get it done. I have a buyer for it when you finish."

"Ron's a nice guy. He goes out to the sound looking for birds," he said. "He knows a lot about them."

"Ridiculous."

Mrs. Dibber put on her blue crocheted shawl and picked up her grocery bag.

"We're out of milk and ziti," she said. "I'm going shopping." She walked through the foyer and out the front door, head up like the elegant owner of a mansion, falling apart or not falling apart.

Mike hurried outside into a blue summer morning and finished caulking the stern of the boat. He had been kind of slow, what with Ron, shooting baskets with Lionel, and sitting along Rachet's trampled grass highway, hoping to see her. He did not know about her home in the boat seat, for she came there by night and was quiet by day, as were the kittens.

He finished caulking, opened the paint bucket, and had sat down on the weedy lawn to stir it when he saw a yellow-and-orange-striped tail swish down from the platform in the bow of the upside-down boat. Only one animal in the world had a tail like that. He kept stirring and thought of what to do. The last time he had seen her, she'd run off when he tried to pet her.

Rachet suddenly leaped to the ground with a kitten in her mouth. She went back for the other two and placed them in a semicircle before Mike.

"Gosh," he exclaimed, "they sure are cute, Rachet." He smiled and went on stirring the paint and admiring the kittens. He complimented their blue eyes and black-and-white fur as well as their whiskers, which came forward to sense him. But mostly he was amazed at Rachet's tameness.

When Mike was done admiring them, Rachet picked up the kittens and returned them to the boat.

That was a kitten debut, he realized. *I saw some African lions on TV put their kittens before the lion pride to show them off. Wow, I am Rachet's pride. That's what this presentation means.* He stopped stirring and pondered. *It's like a girl's debut. The house cat has a coming-out party, too.*

Suddenly Rachet's whiskers twitched and her nostrils widened. Taking in scents as she left the boat she vanished.

Her kittens, now confident after the debut, jumped down from the boat and followed her through the hole in the fence. Before Mike could catch them they had darted into the field and were gone.

He got to his feet, wondering what made Rachet run away, when around the corner of the house strode Ron, the bird expert from the Audubon Society.

"I found another owl pellet yesterday. It was in your front yard," he said as he approached Mike.

"So near," Mike said, inwardly glad Rachet was gone.

"Yeah, it leads me to believe the nest is around here," said Ron. "Have you seen anything spooky and white at night?"

Mike suddenly remembered the large white cloud he had spotted near the tower. It could have been an owl. Was the barn owl Mrs. Dibber's ghost?

"I know you said they nest in barns. Would they nest in the tower of a house?" Mike asked. "There's a broken window up there that it could fly in and out of."

"Good possibility," Ron said, and threw the strap of his camera over his shoulder. "Can we take a look?"

"Come this way," Mike said, and hurried up the outdoor steps, through the kitchen, and up the back stairs to the second floor. Ron was close behind him.

Rachet did not go back to the boat. Ron was an enemy. He was closets and kicks. The kittens were now six weeks old, weaned, and could pounce on mice accurately. It was time to leave them.

Coal Tar tracked Rachet to the briar bush and hid in the edge of the vines, where he rested. The male cardinal screamed at him, defending his youngsters in the stick nest above. They fluttered at the warning. Coal Tar saw the movement and climbed up a thorny stem toward the birds. He pawed, jiggled the branch the nest was on, and put the almost-ready-to-fly nestlings on wing. They flew out of the green briar and landed by the riverside. One nestling on the riverbank fluttered its wings to tell its mother it was hungry.

Delighted, Coal Tar stalked after it. This bird was better than the mice his mother had brought him to play with. Lifting his rear end, he lowered his head and ran toward the fledgling bird. He batted at it, sending it fluttering to the limb of a sycamore tree that leaned over the Olga. His legs stiff, Coal Tar danced sideways on all four paws, then climbed the tree. The bird flew.

Disappointed, he looked down to jump off the limb and saw he was above an island in the river. He miaowed for his mother, lost his grip on the bough, and fell. Landing on all four feet on the reed-edged island, he cried the kitten's "desperation cry."

"Miaow!"

Shifty heard it—and had he not just caught a rabbit, he would have been interested in the cat. Ringx did not hear him, although she was near. She was sleeping in the maple hollow.

Coal Tar ran to the end of the island and back. Roaring water was all around him. He climbed away from it into a willow sapling.

The other two kittens were on their own. The male

had started toward a farm north of Roxville, and the other, a female, had gone to the bicycle path to woo a person. Her wildness was not very deep.

Rachet had done her job, except that Coal Tar was "miaowing" his need for her. Although he should be on his own, a feeling of motherhood in Rachet sparked and burned at that "miaow."

14

While Coal Tar cried for Rachet, Mike was opening the door at the bottom of a once handsome walnut staircase that led up to the tower.

"This way," he said to Ron, and ran up it. Dust rose as he opened a second door to a long-deserted bedroom. Ron pushed wide-eyed Mike aside and circled the room.

"Nothing," he said, and circled the room again to make sure. A bed, once fashionable with its brass pineapple posts, stood at one end of the room. Chairs with horsehair seats were clustered around a table with eagle feet. A wardrobe sat opposite the bed, and beside it was a hand-carved vanity.

"Did you say this is where you heard the weird noises coming from?" Ron asked.

"Yeah, bloodcurdling screams and clicks."

"Exactly right." He pulled back a dusty velvet drape to expose a narrow door. "Here's another door," said Ron. "This tower must have an attic.

"Barn owls love attics as well as barns, if they have access to them. Shall I open this door?"

"Open it," said Mike, and after several yanks Ron was looking at a ladder that led up to the attic.

"Is that broken window in the attic?" he asked as he climbed it. "Must be—there are no broken ones in the bedroom."

"Right," said Mike, now beginning to believe barn owls might have made those strange, eerie screams he had heard in the heating ducts. But no, those screams were humanlike, and the taps were clocklike. He followed Ron, glad that Mrs. Dibber was out shopping and could not see them hunting for an owl's nest in her house. When his and Ron's eyes adjusted, they saw two white ghosts staring at them, their big heads lowered and swinging. An egg they were protecting lay before them.

"Windy, the barn owl!" Mike exclaimed. "And her mate, I guess. Right here."

"Beautiful," Ron whispered.

The pair of spotted white barn owls with their droll monkeylike faces snapped and hissed like wind as they tried to warn these enemies away from their egg.

"It's late for an egg—they usually lay eggs in January or February," Ron said. "This one didn't hatch. It's probably infertile. The owlets that did hatch must have fledged long ago and flown out the broken window."

The owls snapped their beaks, and Mike realized that this sounded like the tapping noise he and Mrs. Dibber had heard in the ducts in the parlor. He hunched back in the shadows and watched the owls open their beaks, protrude their tongues on one side and close them under pressure to make the loud clicks.

"I'll be darned," said Mike.

Windy continued to sway her head and hiss. Ron pointed his camera and clicked. Windy and her mate lifted their wings in threat, as if to fly at the intruders. Mike saw that their snowy white wings spanned almost four feet.

"The ghostlike cloud!" whispered Mike.

"Yeah," Ron answered. "They sure look like ghosts. You should see them when they fly. They are huge, and some think they can be scary. But they're good ghosts. They rid us of varmints."

Ron snapped his camera several times again, and Windy and her mate, now truly alarmed, hissed more furiously to defend their egg.

"This is an important find," Ron said in a low voice. "We better leave. They'll incubate that infertile egg until it breaks. Then they'll fly off to the woods and fields until next nesting season, when they'll want shelter again."

"Let's go," said Mike.

They backed down the ladder to the bedroom, and Ron closed the attic door, pulling the drapes back. He was smiling broadly.

"This is great," said Ron. "Barn owls."

"They're living in the suburbs, here in a house, not a barn," said Mike.

"Yeah. We thought they were disappearing for lack of farms and barns. But this pair is right here with us, eating all the varmints we attract. We've made a new habitat for them." Ron chuckled. "Smart birds—hiding among us."

"So are the red foxes and deer and turkeys," said Mike. "I've seen them."

"And black bears, coyotes, a few moose and opossums, even weasels," added Ron. "They are right here along with us."

"I wonder if I should tell Mrs. Dibber about the owls." Mike rubbed his chin. "She'll fumigate as soon as she hears. She doesn't like animals."

"Fumigate? Do you have to tell her at all?" Ron was horrified that she might kill the wonderful barn owls.

"No, I don't," said Mike. "I don't blame her for thinking we had ghosts. We did hear screaming and tapping—it must have been the owls in the tower. But I'll be worried until they're out of the attic."

"The screaming is a courtship call you heard," Ron said, smiling. "It means there will be owlets."

Mike opened the door to the stairs. "You say they are rare?"

"Yes. And an asset. If she'll exterminate them it's best not to tell her anything at all."

Mike opened the door at the bottom of the stairs and listened for Mrs. Dibber. All was quiet, so he escorted Ron through the wide Victorian hallway to the back steps. They went down them hurriedly.

Outside, Ron sat down to write notes. Mike walked over to the boat and looked under it. Ratchet was gone. The kittens were gone. Not a trace of them remained—except to Queenella. She had smelled Ratchet and her kittens' frantic exodus when she was coming home, by way of the hole in the fence. The removal of the kittens was a warning. She footed it back to her Hunting Spot in the field.

Excited, Ron looked through the pictures in his digital camera.

"I can give a swell barn owl lecture to the Society next week. When they see these pictures they'll all be out here—a city barn owl is our kind of news."

"Ron, could you wait until the owls are gone? I'm not telling Mrs. Dibber till then."

Ron looked at him. Mike wasn't going to tell Mrs. Dibber she had owls in the tower until they were gone, therefore he, Ron, should not tell the bird lovers either.

They high-fived their unspoken agreement.

Then Ron left. Mike looked out over the field.

"Rachet," Mike whispered. "Come back and be my cat. Ron would never hurt you."

15

Mike applied marine paint to the boat he was working on, some blue paint, a cream stripe, and it was finally done. Mrs. Dibber sold it that afternoon. Mike had planned to use his share of the money to buy cat food to lure Rachet back into the basement.

But the next morning Mrs. Dibber said, "I heard what we thought was that ghost in the heating ducts. I wonder if it's the cats. Maybe we should fumigate." Mike almost told Mrs. Dibber then and there that the ghost was barn owls and she must not fumigate. But he did not. He had promised Ron.

Instead he said, "I ought to fix up another boat."

"Good idea," she said enthusiastically.

He paused; she had offered him no money for the work he had done.

"Uh, do you think I could have some of the money

you got for the boat I fixed up?" Mike asked.

"Food is outrageously expensive," she said quickly, meaning that she was using it toward expenses.

"Well, what about my Social Security money from my father, then?" He ignored her remark about food prices.

"Oh yes—I've been saving it for you in a bank account." She smiled like a fox.

"But I can't write out a check," he said. "I want to use the money that I am entitled to."

"I'll write out your checks when you need them. We'll save the rest until you're eighteen. The money will gather interest."

"I want to write my own checks," he said. "My dad meant me to have it to spend."

"Oh," she said somewhat guiltily. "Well. I suppose you can have your own checks. I'll have the bank put your name on them."

He looked into her face. She did not blink or avoid his eyes—he believed her.

Then she turned back to the counter and, cracked some eggs in a bowl.

Mike was elated to hear she was putting his money at

his disposal. He could buy cat food, lots of cat food, and put it behind a tree in the backyard, where Mrs. Dibber never went. He could lure Rachet out of the wilds. Maybe she would let him pet her again; maybe even hold her.

"I'm making scrambled eggs—do you want some?" she asked. Mike told her he had already eaten. He wanted to get outside.

Mrs. Dibber scrambled her eggs and sat down to breakfast.

"The second boat will be beautiful, I know. You do nice work," she said. She had noticed!

Touched by this compliment, Mike closed the kitchen door behind him, walked down the outdoor steps, and got out the sandpaper so he could begin on the second boat. He looked at the hole in the fence through which Rachet came and went. She wasn't there.

"Rachet," he whispered. "Now that I'm part of your pride, will you come to me?" He was sanding the hull of the second boat when around the house came Lionel.

"Hey, Mike," he yelled. "There's a fire truck and a mob of people at the Olga River Bridge. Let's go see."

"A fire truck on the bridge?"

"Some black kitten is stuck on the island and they're trying to rescue it."

Mike pulled the tarp over the boat and followed Lionel. They climbed over his fence, raced across the field to the bridge, and joined the group of people gathered at the railing over the river.

Not far away, Rachet was sunning on the shingles. Her drowsy eyes slanted like the Egyptian cat goddess Bast, her orange and yellow fur blended with the dry grasses of the field. She was half asleep, although her ears were up and listening and her whiskers were wired to all movement. The people on the bridge were trying to rescue Coal Tar. But Rachet would not approach her kitten while so many people were around.

Mike and Lionel leaned on the bridge railing, trying to locate the little black kitten that everyone was talking about. Mike finally saw him in the bouncy willow limbs.

It's one of Rachet kittens. I recognize it, said Mike to himself. Aloud he said, "I wonder how it got there?"

"A hawk dropped her," said Lionel. He assumed, as many do, that all cats are female. "That's the only way a cat could get on an island."

"Maybe an owl," said Mike.

"Maybe someone threw her there," said a man who had overheard them.

"Maybe," said Mike.

"To the left and down," ordered a bulky man, who to the firefighters' amusement was telling them how to do their work.

"Lower it now," called a woman who was also involved in the rescue.

Coal Tar, seeing the ladder coming down, retreated deeper in the willow trees and miaowed a shrill desperation call. It was heard by most of the cats of Roxville Station but was inaudible to the humans.

The observers on the bridge watched tensely as the ladder lowered. It was not long enough! They moaned.

"Now what will we do?" cried a little girl named Troy.

"We've got a kayak," said Derek, one of two high school boys standing next to her. "My brother and I will run the river to the island and grab her."

"Oh, that's great," Troy said.

"We'll get your cat," Derek told her, and ran down the hill toward their boathouse with his brother.

"It's not my cat," Troy called. "But I want it."

At the boat dock, the boys lifted a kayak over their heads and carried it a little distance above the island. There they put it in the water. The crowd cheered.

In no time the boys paddled it close to the island, reached out, and grabbed the willow branches to pull themselves to land. Coal Tar vanished farther into the branches. The water pulled hard on the kayak, the willows broke, and the boys skimmed on down the Olga. Downriver, they hopped out and walked back up carrying their kayak to their put-in spot to try again.

They missed the island by three feet the second time

and pulled out on shore below the bridge to discuss trying it once more.

"Oh, poor little kitten," Troy cried from the bridge. "It's going to get dark soon. What will we do?"

"The water's too swift to wade to the island," a man said.

"And it's gonna get swifter," said a police officer standing beside Troy. "A big storm is coming. They say it will dump six inches, and six inches will almost cover the island."

"We have to do something," Troy cried. "Do something, officer. Do something, plea-z-ze?" The officer shrugged.

"Not worth a human life," he said and walked away.

Troy turned to her dad, a man named Chavez. "I want her, Daddy. She's so sweet. She's only a kitty. I want her," she begged. "Please save her."

Mike could see by Chavez's face that he wanted his daughter to have the kitten, and he envied her that father.

Rachet had heard the shrill ultrasonic sounds of Coal Tar's desperation calls. They rang out above the rescuers' noise and Troy's cry. But the people could not hear the sound. As it grew darker, Rachet answered his call this time by running to a bush near the chipmunk den, not far from the water.

Peering through the leaves, she saw Coal Tar on the island. The water around it was fast and dangerous.

Ice Bucket heard those same "desperation cries" from her nest in the multiflora roses where she was nursing four young. Although the crying kitten was not hers, it was a cat-universal cry and made her anxious. Shaking off her now-satisfied nurslings, she ran to the edge of the wild-rose patch and from there to the river's edge. The boys in the kayak went racing by, their paddles flashing, as they tried a third time to steer in the current. They whooped and laughed. Terrified, Ice Bucket dove under the wild roses and went back to her nest. She curled around her young.

On the third try the boys paddled to the island and grabbed the willows, but before they could beach the boat, it went swirling down the river with the boys holding broken willows in their hands.

A man on the bridge watched the kayak miss the

island for the third time and lowered a basket on a rope. He reasoned that the kitten was hungry and would jump in the basket to get food. The basket dangled off the bridge a good fifteen feet from the island.

Queenella heard but did not care. She was too old. Her time for kittens was over. She was asleep in her First Home in the haunted house basement. She had felt the low pressure of the coming storm and gone to shelter. The officer with his access to the weather radio station and Queenella with her sensitive body were right. The sun disappeared, the sky darkened, and thunder rumbled in the clouds. Coal Tar crawled deeper into the willows.

Big raindrops fell suddenly, sending what was left of the crowd on the bridge running for cover—Mike, Lionel, Troy, and the firefighters among them. Rachet, one eye and ear on Shifty's den, one eye and ear on the island, stayed under the big leaves of a skunk cabbage on the riverbank.

The rain poured all dusk and night. It swept into the river, raising the Olga three inches, then four, then six. Coal Tar climbed higher into the branches of the young willows and shook the rain from his fur. The Olga rose still higher.

At 2 A.M. a two-by-four crashed into the willow trees on the island and jammed against their limbs. A box rammed into the wood and a tumbling, falling-apart boathouse piled up on top of that. The water ran over and around them in torrents. Coal Tar crept off the water-dipping willows and reached a beam in the boat-house attic. Wet and trembling, he watched the deluge all around him.

The night was long. Rachet moved back from the river as it rose but kept her green eyes on the kitten in the attic of the boathouse.

Coal Tar clung to his spot on the beam above. In high decibels, he miaowed.

Around dawn a tree that had been uprooted swept down in the flood and lodged against the boathouse. It blocked the river to one side of the island and reached from the riverbank to the island. Coal Tar "miaowed" again. By then the rain had stopped.

Rachet crept along the water's edge but was frightened back to the leaf-cover by three people. Chavez and his daughter had returned, and they'd brought another man with them. They clumped down the embankment in boots and waterproof gear. Chavez was talking about how he could wade the swift water to the island on a rope if his friend would hold one end.

"This is crazy," said large, red-faced Pete, Chavez's friend. "No cat's worth this."

"My daughter is," said Chavez, and adjusted his coat. They stood by the flooded river, and Chavez took one end of the rope.

At that moment they heard stones roll behind them, and down the slope came Mike. He saw what Chavez and his partner were planning, and fearing for them, looked at the fallen tree and had another idea.

"I'll get the kitten," he said. "Does anyone have a paper bag?"

"I do," said Pete. "I brought my lunch in it."

Mike took it and suddenly, as swiftly as a bird's flight, jumped up on the tree trunk and balanced himself over the roaring water for an instant.

"Don't do it!" shouted Chavez, seeing what he intended. "I'll get her." He waded into the edge of the river, where the rush of the flood nearly knocked him off his feet. He turned back.

Mike, blocking his mind to everything but the fallen tree under his feet, ran swiftly toward the island.

Then Mike's right foot slipped. It was stopped by a tree limb. Grabbing one of the willow trees, he climbed through its limbs above the flooded island to the boat-house.

Chavez and Pete hardly breathed. Troy had squeezed her eyes shut.

"Kitty, kitty," Mike called. Out of a corner of the collapsed structure peeked Coal Tar. The magic of that sound was ancient and undeniable. Mike waited a few minutes, then took the paper bag out of his coat pocket and rattled it open. Holding on to a limb with one hand, he reached out and put the bag on the floor of the ravaged attic. He waited.

Chavez and Pete didn't speak for fear of breaking Mike's concentration. The muddy floodwater swirled under the tree and thundered over most of the island. Mike didn't move.

After long minutes Coal Tar sniffed the bag several

times, then four-legged into it. He danced around inside. Mike picked up bag and kitten. He twisted the bag closed, then let go of the limb and started back to shore on the fallen tree. He ran on the trunk and jumped off on the river shore.

He presented the bag to Chavez.

"Your kitten, sir. I call it Coal Tar. I can't tell its sex."

"Gosh," Chavez said. "That was brave. Thank you, thank you."

Troy, her long hair loose in the wind, grasped bag and kitten. She hugged them close.

"You're amazing," she said to Mike. "I was so scared for you."

"Why? I was in no trouble. Do it all the time."

Troy looked out at the roaring, swollen river and back at Mike.

She took Coal Tar out of the bag and kissed his wet nose. Coal Tar mewed, the meow for humans only.

Mike was fascinated to see that Rachet's kitten was not wild and spitting like she was, but docile and loving. The wild cat in Coal Tar had vanished, blanketed by that wondrous pull of human and cat to live with each other on each one's own terms. He meowed again.

"You've got a good dad," Mike said to Troy, and turned slowly away. It was not food that had domesticated the cat. Cats could get that on their own. He turned back to Troy.

"Give him lots of paper bags and love," he said.

As if in reply Coal Tar said, "Meow."

"Oh, I will, I will," Troy answered back.

In the green briar bush Rachet heard the "meow" and knew her kitten was talking to a human. Coal Tar was telling Troy he would be a loving cat.

The kicks and closets had marred Rachet, but not Coal Tar. He would fill a strange and mysterious need in both human and cat.

Rachet slinked away from the confusion and climbed the maple tree. She sniffed the hollow where Ringx had raised her kits and was pleased to find them gone.

After her raccoon kits were grown, Ringx had deserted the maple hollow to stretch out on the limbs of the big trees in the woods.

Rachet crawled into her hollow and fell asleep, draped like a rag at the entrance.

16

The floodwaters abated and the summer swung on. The daylilies bloomed and went to seed. The Queen Anne's lace began blooming, the goldenrod appeared, and the tree that Mike had walked on across the Olga River became a bridge to the island for squirrels and Shifty.

Windy had left the tower with her mate after the egg was crushed from turning and brooding it. They had returned to a roosting site in the cliffs above the river.

One day Mike sneaked up to the tower attic to check on the owls. Finding them gone and the egg smashed, he thought about fixing the broken window. But the owls, where would they nest next spring? There were no more barns for them in Roxville. This part of the house wasn't used and could well be turned over to the owls. Mrs. Dibber wouldn't give him the money to mend it anyway. So instead of fixing the window he put a piece of plastic on the floor to keep it dry in bad weather.

On the sultry dog days of late summer, while Mike worked hard on another boat, Rachet napped on the cool infrastructure of the bridge and Shifty lounged under the bittersweet vines with its now yellow-green fruits. Ringx was stretched out on the limb of a tree while Lysol stayed in his cool underground den. The young cardinals, long out of their nest but still in a family group, followed their parents to seeds at the bird feeder in the yard where Flea Market lived. They opened their beaks to sweat in the heat.

The milkweeds went to seed, and the black-eyed Susans bloomed like orange-and-black butterflies. The pollywogs in the pools metamorphosed into toads and hopped ashore to find flies and small beetles. Mike spent every summer morning outside, working on the boat.

Mrs. Dibber had given him some money for supplies such as sandpaper, caulking, and paint. And he could write out his very own checks now for canned cat food. He set the cans behind the big maple tree at the edge of the yard, just as he had planned.

And Rachet for her part in the scheme of things simply changed her First Home to a cooler spot. It was closer to the haunted house, under a dead lilac bush by the fence and the big maple tree. The vines that had smothered her bush made it an umbrella of leaves to protect her from rain and sun.

Rachet made a bed beneath it, and unseen by bird, beast, and man, she rolled over on her back by day, paws outstretched. When she was not dozing and Mike was outside working, she pinned her eyes and whiskers on him.

Queenella had remained ensconced in the cool haunted house basement. She lived on the abundant mice near the house and did not even miss the Bent Lady. She had adjusted to the reality of life after the new station was built by hunting for herself, so felt no need to move.

Ice Bucket, on the other hand, moved her First Home from the bushes on the bicycle path to the dense brush by the two sisters' house on Mike's block. From there she had to go through Queenella's territory to get to the field mice. And that took cat-patience. At the end of a night of hunting, she would stop when she came to Queenella's highway and locate the madam through whiskers, eyes, and nose. When Queenella appeared, striding smoothly down her private catwalk, back straight, tail held out, Ice Bucket hissed. Queenella sat down sphinxlike and in plain view of Ice Bucket. Ice Bucket looked away. Then Queenella looked away, and Ice Bucket looked back and Queenella looked away. They seemed to be ignoring each other, but each was very aware of the other's every move. Suddenly, when Ice Bucket was looking away, Queenella dashed over the crossroads and glided home. With that, Ice Bucket arose and calmly crossed Queenella's property. Head down, tail switching, she took her own highway to the brush by the two sisters' house.

One night Queenella was at the bottom of a pile of cardboard boxes when she saw a rat. She crouched. The rat saw her and froze. He knew that when he sat still he became invisible to his enemies.

He was right, Queenella could not see him. But she knew he was there. She waited. The rat waited. Long

minutes went by. The rat scratched a flea and Queenella leaped. With her right paw she scooped the rat to
her. He writhed and bit viciously, his chisel teeth seeking her throat. She rolled to her back, raked him with
her powerful hind feet, and bit into the nape of his
neck. The battle was over. Queenella walked away from
her conquest and sat down. She straightened her fur
and washed her paws to wind down from the excitement
of victory.

Then slowly she arose. She did not get the rat but
instead walked deliberately into the deer swamp. She
was old. She was tired. She curled up in a ball, her paws
over her nose, and never got up again.

Windy flew over her in white silence. An owl's feathers are edged by soft locking feather barbs that make
its flight soundless. She flew on to finally alight on the
tower roof. She triangulated on a sound. It was Volton
walking down Ice Bucket's trail.

Suddenly he caterwauled—a banshee jungle cry, loud
and rending.

It awoke Mrs. Dibber and she sat up in bed. Then
she heard the cry again.

At breakfast she told Mike there really was a ghost near-by. She had heard it scream like a deranged person.

Now, Mike reasoned, was the time.

"Mrs. Dibber," he said. "I have to tell you that there is no ghost. Those screams and taps we heard earlier were barn owls. The male barn owl screams when he is courting the female. Ron, my friend who knows a lot about birds, said so. The taps were the owls snapping their beaks.

"The owls were here, nesting in the tower. They came in through the broken window. They have left the tower. That cry last night was a male cat caterwauling for his female. I heard it, too. The owls are gone."

Alice Dibber stopped buttering her toast, put down her knife, and was silent for several minutes. Then she spread the butter again.

"I wish you would fix the blue boat next," she said, changing the subject abruptly. "We could use it next summer for picnics on the islands in the bay that you and Mr. Dibber used to row to."

———

Fall came. Mike went back to school. Rachet caught mice in the field by night and sunned on the shingles by day. She remained unseen by Mike, even though she lay close to the Vinskis' field-side fence when Mike and Lionel were shooting baskets. On a Saturday in October, when Mike was working on the blue boat, listening to a cricket sing slowly to tell the temperature, he thought he heard Rachet. He had not seen her for a long time and feared someone had adopted her, she was so unusual and beautiful. He missed her dreadfully. Once he thought he had an outdoor pet, but now he was unsure. The cat food he placed carefully behind the maple tree so Mrs. Dibber wouldn't see it had been visited by lots of animals. He could not tell which ones.

Mike hurt. That was foolish. He tried to convince himself that Rachet was only a cat.

He got out the caulking paste, stuffed it between two bottom boards, and sat on the grass to reach the underside of the boat.

Suddenly the nearness of the boy, the light, the winds and air, all came together. Rachet arose and walked calmly out of the umbrella of vines. Mike heard the rustlings of the grass and looked up to see her coming across the yard toward him. Her orange-and-yellow fur shone like sunlight. Her green eyes were pinned on him. Could this be? Did Rachet seek him?

Suddenly she sat down. She looked away. He looked away. Rachet looked back. He looked back. Rachet looked away. Then out of the corner of his eye he saw her run to him, her hind legs level with her shoulders. She was not hunting, and her tail was straight up with no kinks at the tip.

Then Stalin bounded around the corner of the haunted house, dragging his leash. He lunged at Rachet. Rachet swiped at him with her paw, then dove into the crack in the foundation of the haunted house.

"No, Stalin! No! Bad dog, bad dog!"

Mike grabbed Stalin's leash, pulled him around the house and down the sidewalk to the Vinskis'. They were not home, so he dragged him to his kennel.

"No, no, no cat, Stalin," he said as he tied the leash tightly to the ring by the kennel door.

"You have scared her away. Now she will never be mine." He felt awful. "Bad dog. Bad, bad dog."

Stalin wagged his tail, barked, and went into his kennel.

Rachet heard the bark. It sounded far away and said that the dog was leashed and safe. She sat still in the passageway in the wall for a few moments, then calmly left and slipped through the hole in the fence. She took her field highway, now gold-ochre with the pollen-heavy ragweed, and went to the roots beneath the fallen tree. She lay down on her stomach, ears pulled back against her head.

The rest of October Rachet hunted the river edge and made her First Home in the tree roots. Mike looked for Rachet but could not find her.

The wind swirled the fallen leaves, and the south-bound birds took bearing on the rays of the sun, then flew on a beeline for the warmer part of the globe. Mike looked and waited. He thought he might never see Rachet again. He washed the dishes, did his chores, and went to school. But his world was gray.

A late-departing robin winged into the trees near the haunted house and stopped for the night. Suddenly he saw Rachet and flew at her, harassing her with loud cries, telling the wild neighborhood an enemy was here—a cat or fox or hawk. Then as suddenly as he began scolding he stopped. Rachet was out of sight. She was on the seat of the upside-down blue boat to avoid the harassing bird.

Mike got down on the ground to put his tools in the toolbox when out from under the boat came Rachet.

She walked right up to him and rubbed her head against his thigh.

"Meow."

Mike heard the yearning in her voice and took her gently in his arms. He rubbed his head against her head.

"Meow," he said.

With that cat word Rachet no longer coveted the box of rags by the hot water pipes. She had a better First Home—Mike.

A mysterious and loving relationship had begun and would evolve.

Why This Book?

One day my daughter's cat, Trinket, carried her kittens down the staircase and placed them on the rug before us. We admired them as anyone would, and when we were done oohing and ahhing, Trinket carried them back upstairs.

The kittens were on their own from that introduction to society on.

I was enamored. This was a house cat, a loner, not a social animal like the dog. Yet here she was behaving socially and presenting her kittens to us as a lioness presents her cubs to the social pride.

"There is more to a domestic cat than its loner-self," I said to my daughter and started taking notes on *Felis domesticus*.

Years later I came upon a book by a German scientist who had studied the behavior of the domestic cat for twenty years. I learned that cats have highways, hunting spots, and sunning spots. I had noticed this while closely observing the behavior of a group of feral cats around the railroad station at North White Plains where I had twenty minutes to wait while transferring to an express train to New York City. The cats, I wrote, were organized in their own loner way.

Recent cat behavioral scientists have taught me that cats are sensitive animals that are very aware of their environments. With their noses, whiskers, eyes, ears, and bodies, they take in people and their artifacts. When outdoors, they are aware of goldenrod, rivers, trees, butterflies, and storms, as well as the four seasons.

What better animal for me, an environmentalist, to write about than a lovable feral cat who lives outdoors within the wilds?

And Mike, whom Rachet chose as her person—who is he? He is every kid who writes me to say his parents won't let him have a pet for various reasons. I grieve for them and hope that, like Mike, they can have an "outdoor" pet. Preferably a domestic cat that will give and take love while retaining its independence and freedom.

This is a book I had to write.

Jean Craighead George

A Note from Jean Craighead George

The independence of feral cats has always intrigued me. How could they live on their own? There was a group of such cats living around the station where I switched trains to New York. The wait for my train was made exciting by the cats and a lady who came to feed them—not that they needed it. Because of her, however, I was able to observe these remarkable animals. I know how important observation is, in both writing and science. My observations formed the basis of a book I was to write about the cats many years later.

Discussion Points & Activities

- Name the cats that live at Roxville Station. Compare and contrast their personalities. Where do each of the cats live at the end of the book? How have their lives changed?

- Discuss the ranking system among the cats. What does it mean to be in the top position? How does Rachet change her rank?

- Discuss the phrase "cats walk alone." What does this mean? Support your response by finding examples in the novel.

- How do cats communicate with one another? How do they communicate with humans? Does Rachet use a different language to talk to Mike than she does with the other cats?

- Try to communicate with a friend or classmate without using words. Does your body language (movements, gestures, posture) seem like something that an animal would use?

- By reading *The Cats of Roxville Station,* we learn that birds mark their territory by singing to one another instead of fighting. How do other animals mark their territory? How do humans?

- Discuss the mysterious bond that author Jean Craighead George says exists between cats and humans. What signs do you see of this bond between the characters in the novel? How does living in the wild make this bond difficult for Rachet and the other cats of Roxville Station?

- How does Mrs. Dibber change by the end of the novel? What do you think makes her change?

- Jean Craighead George is a renowned naturalist. What have you learned about nature from reading this book?

- After reading *The Cats of Roxville Station*, create a nature journal. Use a section to record your observations of pets and wild animals. What animals are commonly found near your home and school? What do they look, sound, smell, or move like? Include some blank pages where you can draw the animals you see, like Tom Pohrt draws the cats of Roxville Station.